THE COTTAGE WITHIN

Psychological Horror Novel

D. DECKKER

Dinsu Books

Copyright © 2024 D. DECKKER

All rights reserved

The characters and events portrayed in this book are fictitious. Any similarity to real persons, living or dead, is coincidental and not intended by the author.

No part of this book may be reproduced, or stored in a retrieval system, or transmitted in any form or by any means, electronic, mechanical, photocopying, recording, or otherwise, without express written permission of the publisher.

ISBN-13: 9798304834384

Cover design by: D. DECKKER
Printed in the United States of America

Dedication

*To my wife, Subhashini, for your unwavering support and endless inspiration,
and to my daughter, Sasha, for being the light in every shadow.*

This journey would not have been possible without you.

CONTENTS

Title Page
Copyright
Dedication
Preface

Chapter 1: The Call	1
Chapter 2: The Cottage Appears	5
Chapter 3: Inside the Walls	9
Chapter 4: A Visitor's Warning	14
Chapter 5: The Cottage Knows You	18
Chapter 6: Dreams and Shadows	22
Chapter 7: The Cottage's True Shape	26
Chapter 8: The Rift's First Glimpse	30
Chapter 9: The Visitor's Echo	34
Chapter 10: Manifestations	38
Chapter 11: The Rift Expands	42
Chapter 12: The Rift's History	46
Chapter 13: The Keeper	50
Chapter 14: The Cottage Tightens Its Grip	53
Chapter 15: The Door Beyond Reality	57
Chapter 16: The Keeper's Truth	61

Chapter 17: The Dimension's Tests	65
Chapter 18: The Gateway's Pull	69
Chapter 19: The Rift's Hunger	73
Chapter 20: The Keeper Returns	77
Chapter 21: Confronting the Rift	81
Chapter 22: The Rift's Fury	84
Chapter 23: The Final Battle	88
Chapter 24: The Aftermath	92
Chapter 25: The Legacy of the Rift	96
Afterword	101
Acknowledgement	103
About The Author	105
Books By This Author	107

PREFACE

When I first set out to write *The Cottage Within*, I didn't realize how deeply this story would burrow into my mind—and perhaps, into my own fears. It began as a simple idea: an isolated cottage in the woods, a place where reality bends and emotions unravel. But as the story grew, it became something far more personal.

This is a tale about fear, grief, and resilience, but also about the choices we make when faced with the unknown. It's about the shadows we carry within us and the strength we find when we confront them. At its core, this book explores the tension between letting go of pain and holding on to what defines us.

For every twist and turn in Sarah's journey, I found echoes of my own questions and struggles. Perhaps you, too, will see fragments of your own reflections within these pages.

To my wife, Subhashini, and my daughter, Sasha—this story exists because of your unwavering support and light. Thank you for grounding me when the shadows felt too long.

To the reader: step carefully, but don't be afraid to explore. Some doors are meant to be opened, even if we can never quite close them again.

—D. Deckker

CHAPTER 1: THE CALL

The room felt heavier than it should. Sarah sat cross-legged on the worn carpet of her apartment, the faint hum of the city outside barely breaking through the oppressive quiet. In front of her lay a journal, its leather cover cracked and faded with time. Her hands trembled slightly as she traced the initials embossed on the corner—L.T. Liam Thorn. Her brother.

"Why were you so obsessed with this place?" she muttered, flipping open the journal. The scent of aged paper wafted up, mingling with the stale air of her one-bedroom apartment. Liam's handwriting sprawled unevenly across the pages, chaotic and intense. It was a familiar sight—a reminder of the countless nights he'd stayed up, feverishly scribbling about things no one else could see or understand.

Her fingers paused on a particular entry, the ink smudged as though he'd written it in haste:

It's not just a place—it's alive.

Sarah's stomach twisted. She'd dismissed his obsession with "the cottage" as just another one of his manic fixations. He'd always been like that, chasing things that didn't make sense to anyone but him. And now he was gone, leaving behind only questions she'd been too afraid to ask while he was alive.

A folded piece of paper slipped out from between the pages, fluttering to the floor. Sarah picked it up, unfolding it carefully. It was a map, hand-drawn and crude, marked with cryptic symbols she didn't recognize. Her gaze caught on a set of coordinates scrawled in the corner, barely legible.

"This is ridiculous," she whispered, dropping the map onto the journal. But her eyes lingered, drawn to the symbols. Something about them tugged at her memory, a faint echo of familiarity.

The sharp ring of her phone shattered the stillness. She jumped, her heart hammering. Scrambling to grab it, she saw her best friend Clara's name flash across the screen.

"Hey," Sarah said, her voice hoarse.

"You okay?" Clara's tone was cautious, as if she already knew the answer.

"Yeah, just... going through Liam's stuff." Sarah hesitated. "He had this journal. It's full of... weird things."

"Weird how?"

Sarah looked down at the map again. "He was obsessed with finding this cottage. He thought it was some... I don't know. Magical place, or something."

Clara was silent for a moment. "And you're thinking about looking for it?"

"No," Sarah said quickly, too quickly. "It's just... the symbols. I think I've seen them before. On a hike a few months ago."

Clara sighed. "Sarah, you're not responsible for what happened to him. You know that, right?"

Sarah swallowed hard, her throat tight. "I know."

But she didn't believe it.

The map sat propped against her dashboard, the journal beside it. Sarah gripped the steering wheel tightly, her knuckles white. The coordinates had led her to a remote stretch of highway, bordered by dense forest on either side. The trees loomed tall and ancient, their branches intertwining to form a canopy that blotted out the sun.

"Great, Sarah," she muttered to herself. "Drive into the woods alone to chase a ghost. Smart."

She pulled onto a narrow dirt road that barely seemed wide enough for her car. The deeper she drove, the stranger the world around her became. The trees seemed to shift when she wasn't looking, their gnarled roots clawing at the edges of the road. Shadows flickered in her peripheral vision, but every time she turned her head, there was nothing there.

Her heart pounded as she checked the journal again. Liam had written about this place in fragmented, feverish sentences:

The air feels different here. Thicker. It watches you.

She rolled down her window, and a damp, earthy scent filled the car. He was right. The air did feel different, heavy and charged, like it was waiting for something.

The road ended abruptly at a clearing, the ground littered with moss and fallen leaves. She parked and stepped out, the crunch of her boots unnaturally loud in the silence. There was no birdsong, no rustle of small animals in the underbrush. Just the faint rustling of leaves, though there was no wind.

Sarah unfolded the map again, her hands shaking. The symbols seemed to shimmer in the fading light, almost as if they were alive. She turned in a slow circle, comparing the clearing to the sketch on the page.

"This can't be it," she whispered. But the journal's entry flashed into her mind:

The cottage finds you when it's ready.

The sun dipped below the horizon, casting the clearing in shadow. Sarah's breath quickened as she realized just how far she was from anyone or anything. The forest seemed to close in around her, the trees leaning closer, their twisted branches clawing at the sky.

And then she saw it.

At first, she thought her eyes were playing tricks on her. A faint outline shimmered at the edge of the clearing, barely visible in the gloom. She took a hesitant step forward, and the outline solidified. The cottage stood there, small and unassuming, its dark wooden exterior blending into the surrounding forest. It hadn't been there a moment ago.

Her chest tightened as a cold wave of fear and wonder washed over her. She glanced back at her car, suddenly desperate to leave. But the cottage seemed to call to her, its windows glowing faintly, like eyes watching her every move.

The journal's words echoed in her mind, a whisper carried on the still air:

It's alive.

CHAPTER 2: THE COTTAGE APPEARS

It looked like something out of a fairy tale, small and quaint, with weathered wooden walls and a steep, shingled roof. A thin wisp of smoke curled lazily from the chimney, though there was no sign of life. The windows glimmered faintly, their glass catching the light in a way that felt unnatural, almost sentient. The surrounding trees formed a perfect circle around the clearing, their twisted branches arching overhead like a protective dome.

Sarah's heart pounded as she took a hesitant step forward.

"This can't be real," she muttered. Her voice trembled, barely audible. "It's like something out of a dream."

But the cottage was real. She could feel it, an almost magnetic pull drawing her closer. The air was heavier here, charged with an energy that made her skin prickle. The journal's words echoed in her mind: *It's alive.*

The clearing seemed to shrink as she approached, the trees pressing closer. Her eyes darted around, scanning for movement, but the woods remained still, suffocating in their silence. She stopped a few feet from the cottage, her gaze drawn to the stone foundation. Symbols—the same ones from the map—were carved into the stone, their edges glowing faintly as though lit from within. Her breath quickened.

She crouched down, tracing one of the symbols with her fingertips. It was warm, pulsing faintly under her touch like a heartbeat. A shiver ran through her, and she pulled her hand back, wiping it on her jeans.

"Liam, what did you find?" she murmured.

The door loomed before her, its dark wood streaked with deep grooves, as if it had weathered centuries of storms. She reached out hesitantly, her fingers hovering over the handle. It was smooth and cool at first, but as she wrapped her hand around it, the metal grew warm, almost alive.

"Hello?" she called, her voice barely above a whisper.

A faint sound, almost like a laugh, drifted from the woods behind her. She spun around, her heart hammering. There was nothing there. The trees stood still, their shadows long and unnervingly straight. Sarah clenched her jaw and turned back to the door.

"You came all this way," she muttered under her breath. "Stop being a coward."

Taking a deep breath, she pushed the door open.

Warmth enveloped her the moment she stepped inside, a stark contrast to the damp chill of the forest. The air was thick with the scent of lavender, undercut by something metallic and faintly sour. It wasn't unpleasant, but it set her on edge, like the feeling of static before a storm.

The door creaked shut behind her, the sound unnaturally loud in the stillness. She froze, her pulse quickening, but the room remained empty. Her eyes swept over the interior, taking in the cozy yet unsettling scene. A small living room stretched out before her, its furnishings simple and outdated. An overstuffed armchair sat by the fireplace, its fabric worn and faded. A small wooden table was set for one, a steaming cup of tea resting on its surface.

A kettle hissed faintly on the stove in the adjoining kitchen, though no one was there to tend to it. The walls were lined with shelves filled with books and trinkets, each item meticulously placed, as though someone had been expecting her.

"This doesn't make any sense," she whispered. Her voice sounded foreign in the space, as though it didn't belong.

Her gaze was drawn to the fireplace, where a single photograph sat on the mantle. She stepped closer, her stomach twisting in knots. The photograph was old, its edges yellowed with time. It showed two children—a boy and a girl—standing in front of the very cottage she was in now. The boy's face was unmistakable. It was Liam, his wide grin frozen in time.

Sarah's knees buckled, and she grabbed the edge of the mantle to steady herself. "No," she whispered. "This can't be here. This... this isn't possible."

The sound of footsteps echoed from upstairs.

Her breath hitched, and she spun around, her eyes darting to the staircase in the corner of the room. The footsteps were faint, deliberate, as though someone was pacing just out of sight.

"Hello?" she called, her voice breaking. The footsteps stopped.

The silence pressed down on her, heavy and suffocating. She took a hesitant step toward the stairs, every instinct screaming at her to run. But something rooted her in place, a morbid curiosity or perhaps the same force that had drawn her to the cottage in the first place.

"Who's there?" she demanded, her voice trembling. She waited, but no answer came.

The air grew colder, and the faint scent of lavender was replaced by something sharper, more acrid. The kettle on the stove let out a shrill whistle, the sound piercing the quiet like a scream. Sarah flinched, her heart racing.

"Get it together," she muttered, backing away from the stairs. She turned toward the door, her hand reaching for the handle. It wouldn't budge. The metal was ice-cold now, burning her palm.

The footsteps resumed, slower this time, as if whoever—or whatever—was upstairs was deliberately taunting her. The kettle's whistle grew louder, echoing through the small space until it was almost deafening.

Sarah clapped her hands over her ears, her breaths coming in shallow gasps. And then, just as suddenly as it started, the noise stopped. The silence that followed was even more terrifying.

She turned back toward the staircase, her eyes wide and unblinking. The shadows at the top of the stairs seemed to move, shifting and writhing like they had a life of their own.

"Liam?" she whispered, her voice barely audible. The shadows stilled.

Something creaked above her, a floorboard groaning under unseen weight. Sarah took a step back, her legs trembling. She didn't know what she expected to find, but she couldn't shake the feeling that the cottage was alive, its very walls watching her every move.

CHAPTER 3: INSIDE THE WALLS

The warmth of the cottage clung to Sarah like a heavy, suffocating blanket. Every step she took across the wooden floor creaked louder than it should have, the sound swallowed by the thick, expectant silence. Her fingers brushed against the walls as she moved, almost as if she needed to confirm they were real—solid.

The first room she entered was the rustic kitchen. A stove stood in the corner, its iron surface gleaming faintly despite its aged appearance. Wooden shelves lined the walls, stacked neatly with jars of dried herbs, canned goods, and dishes that looked untouched for decades. Her eyes lingered on the small table in the center of the room. It was set for one, a plate of bread and a steaming mug of tea resting on its surface.

The tea smelled fresh. She leaned closer, hesitating, her breath catching in her chest.

"Hello?" she called again, her voice faltering. Only silence greeted her.

She backed away, her gaze scanning the rest of the room. There was something unsettling about how perfect everything was, as though someone had prepared for her arrival and then vanished just moments before she stepped inside.

"This can't be real," she muttered, clutching her arms. "Someone's messing with me."

The next room she entered was a library. It was larger than it should have been, given the size of the cottage she'd seen from the outside. Shelves stretched from floor to ceiling, filled with books bound in dark leather, their spines embossed with titles in languages she couldn't recognize. Some looked like they might crumble at the slightest touch, their pages yellowed with age, while others seemed almost new, their covers glistening in the dim light.

One book lay open on a nearby table. The pages were covered in intricate symbols and diagrams, spiraling patterns that made her head throb if she stared at them too long. She closed the book quickly, her fingers trembling.

A mirror hung on the far wall, its surface warped and tarnished. As she approached, her reflection came into view—but something was wrong. The woman in the mirror moved differently, her motions a fraction of a second out of sync with Sarah's own. She froze, staring at the image as a cold wave of fear washed over her.

"Stop," she whispered. Her reflection did not.

Her breath hitched, and she turned away, her heart pounding.

Further exploration led her to a small bedroom. The bed was neatly made, the quilt draped perfectly over the edges. A wooden dresser stood against the wall, its drawers slightly ajar. Sarah opened one, finding a collection of old photographs. They were all of the same two children she'd seen in the photograph on the mantle. Liam and the girl.

But the photos were strange. In some, the children looked happy, playing in the yard outside the cottage. In others, they stared directly at the camera, their faces solemn and pale. The background in each photo remained eerily static—the same trees, the same gray sky, as though time had frozen around them.

Sarah's fingers brushed against something at the bottom of the drawer. She pulled it out and found a small music box. Its wooden surface was etched with swirling patterns that matched the symbols on the map. She opened it hesitantly, and a hauntingly familiar melody filled the air.

It was a tune from her childhood, one her mother used to hum to soothe her to sleep. Tears pricked at the corners of her eyes, the ache of nostalgia twisting into something darker.

"No," she whispered, snapping the box shut. She shoved it back into the drawer and stepped away, her breaths coming in shallow gasps. "This isn't happening."

The hallway stretched longer than it should have, the floorboards creaking under her weight. The walls seemed closer now, the shadows deeper. At the end of the hall stood a door. It was different from the others, its dark wood scarred with deep grooves. There was no keyhole, no handle—only the faint outline of a doorframe etched with symbols.

She pressed her ear against the wood, straining to hear. Faint murmurs drifted through, too soft to make out the words but unmistakably human. Her hand rested on the door; her fingers splayed across the rough surface.

"If you're going to stay here," she muttered to herself, "you need to know what's behind that door."

She pushed her shoulder digging into the wood. It didn't budge. Frustration bubbled up inside her, and she slammed her fist against the door.

"Come on!" she shouted. The echoes of her voice seemed to linger, bouncing back at her from every direction.

The murmurs behind the door stopped.

Sarah retreated to the living room; her nerves frayed. The photograph on the mantle still stared back at her, an unspoken reminder of how little she understood. She sank into the overstuffed armchair by the fireplace, the cushions sagging under her weight. The heat of the fire did little to calm the chill that had settled in her bones.

She tried to piece everything together, her thoughts racing. Liam had been obsessed with this place, convinced it held answers to questions only he seemed to know. And now she was here, chasing his ghost, trapped in a house that seemed to defy reason.

Her eyelids grew heavy as exhaustion took over. Despite the fear clawing at the edges of her mind, she drifted off, the crackling of the fire lulling her into an uneasy sleep.

In her dream, she was back in the forest. The trees loomed taller, their branches reaching out like hands. Liam's voice called to her, faint and desperate.

"Sarah, help me."

She turned toward the sound, her feet moving from their own accord. The trees parted, revealing a clearing. The cottage was in its center, but it was wrong now. Its walls bled black tar, and the windows were dark, gaping holes. The door creaked open, and she saw Liam standing inside, his face pale and his eyes hollow.

"Sarah," he said again, his voice breaking. "Please."

She woke with a start, her chest heaving. The room was dark, the fire was reduced to glowing embers. Her gaze darted to the table in front of her, and her breath caught.

A small object sat in the center of the table. It hadn't been there before.

Her hands trembled as she reached for it, her fingers closing around a small, worn key. She recognized it instantly. It was the key to her childhood diary, a long-lost keepsake she hadn't seen in years.

The whispers started again, soft and insistent. They seemed to come from all around her, echoing off the walls. She turned toward the hallway, her heart sinking as her eyes landed on the door at the end.

It was open.

Just a crack, but enough to see the inky darkness beyond.

Sarah's grip tightened on the key, her knuckles white. The whispers grew louder, calling her forward. The room seemed to tilt, the shadows stretching toward her like fingers. She took a shaky step toward the hallway, her pulse pounding in her ears.

The cottage waited.

CHAPTER 4: A VISITOR'S WARNING

The hallway felt colder than it had moments before, as though the air itself was recoiling from Sarah's presence. She stood frozen, staring at the door at the end of the hall. It was still slightly ajar, the inky darkness beyond it beckoning her like an open wound. Her fingers tightened around the small key she had found, its cold metal biting into her palm.

With a deep breath, she forced her legs to move. Each step toward the door felt heavier than the last, as though the floor itself was resisting her approach. The whispers that had called her earlier had quieted, replaced by an unnerving silence that pressed against her eardrums. She stopped a few feet away from the door, her breath shallow and uneven.

She reached out tentatively, nudging the door open with the tips of her fingers. But instead of swinging inward, it refused to budge. Something invisible and unyielding held it in place, the gap remaining no wider than a crack. Sarah pressed her ear against the rough wood, straining to hear anything beyond the oppressive silence.

And then she noticed them. Scratches.

They were faint at first, barely noticeable against the dark wood of the floor. But as Sarah's eyes adjusted, she saw them more clearly: jagged, erratic lines etched into the surface. The markings radiated outward from the door like the desperate claw marks of something trying to escape. Or something trying to get in.

Her stomach churned as she crouched to get a closer look. Among the scratches, she spotted a series of symbols, faint but deliberate, carved into the wood with more precision. They were eerily similar to the ones she had seen on the map and the foundation of the cottage. Her fingertips hovered over them, the grooves feeling almost warm to the touch. A faint hum seemed to emanate from the markings, resonating deep within her chest.

Nearby, something glinted in the dim light. Sarah's gaze darted into a small, battered notebook lying just to the side of the door. The leather cover was cracked and peeling, its edges worn smoothly from years of handling. She hesitated, the air around her growing heavier as though the very cottage was holding its breath.

She picked it up.

The notebook's pages were yellow and brittle, the ink smudged in places as though written in haste. She flipped through it, her pulse quickening as she read the frantic scrawl within:

Day 3: The cottage isn't normal. The rooms change when I'm not looking. The windows show places I've never been to. It knows what I'm thinking.

Day 5: Time doesn't move right here. I swear I've been here for weeks, but my watch says it's only been hours.

Day 7: I can hear it now. The whispers. They're louder at night. They're coming from the door at the end of the hall.

Sarah's breath hitched as she flipped to the final page. The handwriting had grown messier, almost illegible:

If you're reading this, leave now. It knows you're here.

She snapped the notebook shut, her hands trembling. The words clawed at her mind, their weight settling heavily in her chest. A cold sweat broke out along the back of her neck as she stood, clutching the notebook tightly against her side. Her eyes darted back to the locked door, its dark surface now seeming more sinister than before.

"This is ridiculous," she muttered, shaking her head. "Just some paranoid ramblings. Some crackpot conspiracy theorist was here before me. Nothing to worry about."

The sound of her own voice felt hollow, a flimsy shield against the growing dread that coiled in her stomach. She wanted to believe the words, to dismiss the warning as the delusions of someone who'd been too isolated for too long. But her fingers wouldn't release the notebook, clutching it like a lifeline.

"It's just a coincidence," she said, louder this time, as though that might make it true. The symbols, the scratches, the whispers—it was all just… a coincidence. Wasn't it?

Sarah returned to the living room; the notebook still clutched tightly in her hands. The fire in the hearth had died down to faintly glowing embers, casting flickering shadows across the walls. She dropped into the armchair by the fireplace, the cushions sagging under her weight. The room felt different now, heavier, as though the very air had thickened.

She flipped open the notebook again, unable to stop herself from reading more. The words pulled at her, each sentence sinking hooks into her mind. The writer's growing desperation seeped through the pages, and with each new entry, Sarah felt the walls of the cottage pressing closer.

The whispers began again.

Soft at first, like the faint rustle of leaves. But they grew louder, more insistent, weaving through the cracks in her thoughts. She clutched the arms of the chair, her knuckles white, her breath shallow.

"Stop it," she whispered, squeezing her eyes shut. The whispers didn't obey. They wrapped around her, pulling her attention back to the hallway.

Her eyes snapped open, her gaze darting toward the door at the end of the hall. The whispers seemed to emanate from it, their tone urgent and pleading. She stood, her legs trembling as though the floor itself had grown unstable. The firelight flickered erratically, casting grotesque shapes across the walls.

"What do you want?" she demanded, her voice cracking. The whispers didn't answer, but the intensity of their pull increased, dragging her back toward the hallway.

The hallway was darker than before, the shadows pooling like ink at the edges. The door loomed ahead, the faint murmurs behind it growing louder with each step Sarah took. Her hand shook as she reached for the key she'd found earlier, now warm against her palm. But as she approached, the whispers suddenly stopped.

The silence was deafening. Sarah froze, her chest tight as she stared at the door. There was a handle. It was not there before. Then, with a sharp *click*, the handle jiggled.

She stumbled back, her pulse pounding in her ears. The handle twisted slowly, as though something on the other side was testing it, teasing her. Her back hit the wall, her breath coming in shallow gasps. The door didn't open, but the shadows around it seemed to ripple, shifting like something alive.

"No," she whispered, shaking her head. Her voice was barely audible over the sound of her heartbeat. "No, this isn't real."

The handle jiggled again, harder this time, and the wood groaned under the strain. Sarah bolted, her footsteps echoing loudly as she fled back to the living room.

For a moment, everything was still. The only sound was the ragged cadence of her breathing. But in the back of her mind, she knew the cottage wasn't done with her yet.

CHAPTER 5: THE COTTAGE KNOWS YOU

Sarah woke to sunlight streaming through the windows, warm and golden as it painted soft patterns across the wooden floor. She blinked against the brightness, momentarily disoriented. The events of the night before hovered at the edges of her memory like a dream she couldn't shake. Her body ached, her limbs heavy with exhaustion, but something about the light felt wrong. Too warm. Too golden.

She sat up slowly, her eyes darting to the clock on the mantle. The hands were frozen, pointing to the exact moment she'd entered the cottage. Her stomach twisted.

"How long have I been here?" she murmured, her voice breaking the oppressive silence. "Just one night… right?"

The fire in the hearth had burned down to cold ashes, yet the room was bathed in an unnatural glow. Sarah swung her legs over the side of the armchair, the floor creaking beneath her feet. She glanced toward the hallway where the locked door waited, but the thought of approaching it made her stomach churn. For now, she needed to move—to prove to herself that this place wasn't alive.

The kitchen was exactly as she'd left it, or at least it appeared to be. The kettle sat cold and still on the stove, its surface gleaming faintly in the morning light. The table, however, caught her eye. A small wooden box sat at its center; one she hadn't noticed before.

Sarah's breath caught as she approached. The box was familiar—too familiar. Her fingers trembled as she lifted the lid, revealing its contents: a stack of old letters tied with twine, a small stuffed bear missing one button eye, and a photograph tucked carefully beneath them. She pulled the photograph out with shaking hands.

It was of her and Liam, taken when they were children. They sat side by side on the front steps of their childhood home, their smiles wide and carefree. She hadn't seen this picture in years, and yet here it was, perfectly preserved.

"How did this get here?" she whispered, her voice barely audible. Her fingers tightened around the edges of the photo. "I didn't bring this. I couldn't have. Infact I didn't had this with me."

The stuffed bear and letters stared back at her like ghosts from a past she'd tried to bury. The box smelled faintly of cedar, the scent tugging at memories she wasn't ready to face. Tears pricked at the corners of her eyes, but she wiped them away angrily.

"No," she said, her voice firm. "This isn't real."

As she stood, the photograph still clutched tightly in her hand, a faint sound reached her ears. Her heart skipped a beat. It was a voice—soft, barely audible, but unmistakable. Her name.

"Sarah..."

Her chest tightened as she turned toward the sound. It was coming from the hallway, from behind the locked door. The voice was faint but familiar, tugging at her heart in a way that was both comforting and terrifying.

"Liam?" she whispered, her voice trembling. The photograph slipped from her fingers, fluttering to the floor. She stepped toward the hallway, her legs heavy as though the air itself resisted her movement.

The voice called again, clearer this time. "Sarah... help me."

Her breath quickened as she reached the door. The symbols carved into its surface seemed to shimmer in the golden light, pulsing faintly as though alive. She pressed her ear against the wood, straining to hear. The voice was gone, replaced by a deep, suffocating silence.

Her fingers brushed against the door handle, the cold metal sending a shiver up her arm. She twisted it, but the door wouldn't budge. Frustration bubbled up inside her, and she banged her fist against the wood.

"Liam are you in there?" she shouted. Her voice echoed down the hallway, unanswered.

The light in the room shifted suddenly, growing dimmer. Shadows crept along the walls, twisting and writhing like living things. Sarah backed away from the door, her heart racing. The floor beneath her feet groaned, a low, ominous sound that seemed to reverberate through her chest.

The voice returned, louder this time, but distorted. It sounded like Liam, but it was wrong.

"Sarah... come closer."

Her stomach lurched, and she stumbled back further, her hands clutching at the walls for support. The air grew colder, the warmth of the golden light replaced by a bone-deep chill. The whispers she'd heard the night before returned, overlapping and urgent, their unintelligible words forming a cacophony that pressed against her skull.

"Stop it!" she cried, covering her ears. The whispers only grew louder, filling the space around her until she thought her head might split open.

The lights flickered violently, plunging the hallway into darkness before returning in bursts of dim, erratic light. The floor beneath her feet felt unsteady, as though the very cottage was shifting, breathing.

Sarah bolted back to the living room, her chest heaving. The box still sat on the kitchen table, its contents untouched, but the photograph she'd dropped was nowhere to be seen. She collapsed into the armchair, her fingers digging into the worn fabric as she tried to steady her breathing.

"What do you want from me?" she whispered, her voice breaking. The cottage didn't answer, but the silence that followed was almost worse. It was thick and expectant, as though the walls themselves were waiting for her next move.

Her gaze darted to the mantle, where the clock still pointed to the exact moment she'd arrived. Time wasn't moving here, not in the way it should. She glanced out the window, but the golden light had faded, replaced by a dim, featureless gray. The forest beyond the glass seemed closer, the twisted branches reaching toward the house as though trying to claw their way inside.

She felt the photograph before she saw it. It was cold against her hand, resting on the arm of the chair. Her blood ran cold as she picked it up. The image had changed.

In the photo, she and Liam still sat on the front steps of their childhood home, but their smiles were gone. Their faces were pale, their eyes hollow and sunken. Behind them, the house was dark, its windows like empty sockets.

Sarah's hands shook as she dropped the photograph onto the floor. It landed face-up, the distorted image staring back at her. She looked away, her breath coming in shallow gasps. The whispers began again, low and insistent, pulling her gaze back toward the hallway.

"No," she said, her voice trembling. "I won't go back there."

But the whispers didn't stop. They grew louder, more demanding, until they drowned out every other thought. The floor beneath her creaked, the sound rhythmic and deliberate, like footsteps. The air grew heavier, pressing against her chest until she could barely breathe.

The cottage was alive, and it knew her.

CHAPTER 6: DREAMS AND SHADOWS

Sarah's eyelids grew heavier with each passing second. Despite the fear gnawing at her, exhaustion finally claimed to her as she slumped into the armchair. The room's oppressive silence seemed to wrap around her, lulling her into a restless sleep.

In her dream, she stood at the edge of a vast, otherworldly landscape. The ground beneath her feet shimmered like liquid glass, shifting and swirling with each step. Towers of crystalline light stretched endlessly into the dark sky, their forms flickering between solid and intangible. The air buzzed with a low hum that seemed to resonate inside her chest.

And there, on the horizon, stood Liam.

His figure was faint, almost translucent, but unmistakable. He turned toward her, his expression calm yet distant. The sight of him pulled at her heart, a mixture of relief and anguish flooding her chest. She tried to call out to him, but her voice caught in her throat.

"It's beautiful here," Liam said, his voice soft and echoing, as though it came from all around her. He reached out a hand, his eyes locking with hers. "Don't be afraid."

Her feet moved without her permission, carrying her closer to him. But no matter how far she walked, the distance between them didn't close. The landscape began to shift around her, the towers of light bending and dissolving into swirling shadows. Liam's form grew fainter, his hand still outstretched.

"Liam, wait!" she finally managed to cry, her voice cracking.

But he disappeared, his figure swallowed by the shadows.

Sarah jolted awake, her chest heaving. The room was bathed in dim, gray light, the fire long since extinguished. Her heart raced as she tried to shake off the remnants of the dream, the vivid image of Liam's outstretched hand lingering in her mind.

She rubbed her arms, her skin clammy and cold. Something drew her attention to the window. A faint handprint was pressed into the condensation on the glass, perfectly formed and unmistakable. It was larger than hers, its edges smudged as though someone had drawn it there moments before.

Her pulse quickened as she backed away, her eyes darting to the locked door at the end of the hallway.

"It's just condensation," she whispered, her voice trembling. "Nothing more."

But deep down, she didn't believe it.

The shadows in the cottage seemed to deepen as the day dragged on, the light from the windows growing dim and pale. Sarah paced the living room, her thoughts a whirlwind of fear and confusion. She couldn't stop glancing at the notebook, its frayed edges practically calling out to her.

As she passed the mirror on the wall, something caught her eye. She froze, her breath hitching. The shadows on the walls didn't align with the furniture. One stretched too far, its edges jagged and wrong, moving ever so slightly despite the stillness of the room.

"No," she muttered, stepping back. "It's just my mind playing tricks on me. That's all this is. A trick."

The shadow shifted again, creeping closer to her. She stumbled backward, her hands gripping the edge of the table for support. The air grew colder, and the faint scent of lavender was replaced by something acrid and sharp.

"Stop it," she hissed, her voice shaking.

The shadow stilled, melting back into the wall as though it had never moved. But Sarah couldn't shake the feeling that it was still watching her, waiting for her to let her guard down.

Desperate for answers, Sarah grabbed the notebook and flipped through its pages. Her fingers trembled as she scanned the frantic scrawls, looking for anything she might have missed. Her eyes landed on a recurring symbol; one she hadn't noticed before. It was carved into the corners of nearly every page, its intricate lines forming a spiraling pattern.

Her stomach turned as she realized she'd seen the same symbol etched into the walls of the cottage. It was faint, hidden beneath layers of grime, but unmistakable. The connection sent a chill down her spine.

"What does it mean?" she whispered, tracing the symbol with her finger. The lines seemed to pulse faintly under her touch, as though the notebook itself was alive.

The firelight flickered suddenly, casting the room into darkness for a brief moment before reigniting. Sarah's breath quickened as the whispers began again, low and insistent, filling the room with their eerie cadence.

"No," she said, shaking her head. "I won't let you get to me."

But the whispers grew louder, drowning out her thoughts. They pulled at her, dragging her mind toward the locked door at the end of the hallway. She clenched her fists, her nails digging into her palms as she fought the urge to run.

"I need to know the truth," she said, her voice trembling but firm. "No matter what it takes."

She stood, her resolve hardening as she gripped the notebook tightly. The shadows seemed to pulse around her, alive with anticipation. But Sarah refused to back down. She turned toward the hallway, her steps steady despite the fear clawing at her chest.

CHAPTER 7: THE COTTAGE'S TRUE SHAPE

Sarah stared at the hallway, its dim light barely illuminating the warped wood beneath her feet. Something had changed overnight; the air felt heavier, charged with an electric tension that prickled her skin. She needed to get out. The oppressive weight of the cottage pressed against her chest, and every fiber of her being screamed for her to run. But as she turned to head back toward the front door, her steps faltered.

The hallway stretched endlessly before her.

She froze, her breath catching in her throat. It had been short before, just a few steps to the main room, but now it extended impossibly long, the far end swallowed by shadow. Her pulse quickened as she looked back toward the locked door. It was still there, ominous and waiting, but the distance between her and it now felt insurmountable.

"This isn't happening," she muttered, her voice trembling. "It's just... a dream. I'll wake up."

She stepped forward cautiously, each footfall echoing unnaturally loud. The air grew colder the farther she walked, and the shadows seemed to shift and stretch in her peripheral vision. She kept her eyes fixed ahead, determined to reach the end of the hallway. But when she finally reached the door, her stomach dropped.

She was back where she started.

"No," she whispered, spinning around. The hallway behind her was exactly the same, stretching endlessly in both directions. Every door she opened led her back to the same hallway, the same locked door mocking her at every turn. Her breaths came faster, her chest tightening with panic.

"Stop it," she shouted, slamming her fists against the wall. "Let me out!"

The walls didn't answer, but the shadows seemed to ripple, as though amused by her desperation. She slid down to the floor, her head in her hands, the cold seeping into her skin.

After what felt like hours, Sarah forced herself to stand. Her legs wobbled beneath her, but she steadied herself against the wall. She couldn't stay here, trapped in this endless loop. She turned toward the nearest window, desperate for any sense of normalcy. But as her gaze settled on the glass, her heart stopped.

The forest was gone.

Instead, the world beyond the window had been replaced by a vast, alien landscape. Shimmering plants with translucent leaves swayed in a wind she couldn't feel. The sky above was a swirling mass of colors, shifting and bleeding into one another like oil on water. Strange, flickering shapes moved at the edges of her vision, too quick and indistinct to make out clearly.

Her stomach churned, and she stumbled back from the window, her mind struggling to comprehend what she was seeing.

"This can't be real," she whispered, shaking her head. "This can't be real."

The cottage groaned around her, the sound low and guttural, like the growl of a living creature. The floorboards beneath her feet seemed to shift, tilting slightly, and she grabbed onto the wall for support. Her reflection in the window flickered, distorting for a brief moment before snapping back into place.

The whispers returned, louder now, their tone almost mocking. They seemed to come from every direction, overlapping in a chaotic symphony that made her head throb. She pressed her hands over her ears, but the sound burrowed into her mind, relentless and inescapable.

And then, it laughed.

It started as a low chuckle, deep and resonant, vibrating through the walls. It grew louder, more menacing, until it echoed through the entire cottage. Sarah collapsed to her knees; her hands still pressed against her ears as tears streamed down her face.

"Stop it!" she screamed, her voice cracking. "Just stop!"

The laughter abruptly stopped, leaving behind a suffocating silence. Sarah's breath came in ragged gasps as she lifted her head. The cottage felt different now, as though it was watching her with newfound amusement.

She staggered to her feet, her legs trembling. The hallway seemed to have returned to its normal length, the front door visible just a few steps away. Relief flooded her, and she stumbled toward it, her hand reaching for the handle. But just as her fingers brushed the metal, a loud creak echoed from behind her.

She turned slowly, dread coiling in her stomach.

The locked door at the end of the hallway was now slightly ajar, a sliver of inky darkness visible through the gap. The symbols carved into their surface pulsed faintly, casting eerie shadows across the walls.

Sarah's heart pounded as she took a hesitant step toward the door. The whispers had returned, softer now, coaxing her forward. The air grew colder with each step, her breath visible in the dim light. She stopped just outside the door, her hand hovering over the edge.

"Liam?" she whispered, her voice trembling.

The shadows beyond the door shifted, but no answer came. She stared into the darkness, her mind racing with equal parts fear and curiosity. Something was waiting for her on the other side, something she couldn't ignore.

With a deep breath, she pushed the door open.

CHAPTER 8: THE RIFT'S FIRST GLIMPSE

The door creaked open slowly, the sound low and mournful as though the wood itself resisted her touch. A faint, pulsating light spilled through the widening gap, casting rhythmic shadows that danced across the hallway walls. Sarah froze, her hand still on the handle. The air beyond the door felt different—denser, electric, and cold enough to make her breath visible.

"Sarah..."

The voice was soft, distant, but unmistakable. Liam. It echoed faintly, each syllable carried by the charged air, tugging at something deep inside her. Her chest tightened, her pulse quickening.

"Sarah," the voice said again, clearer this time. "It's okay. Come closer."

Her legs moved of their own accord, her feet carrying her forward even as her mind screamed at her to stop. The light beyond the door grew brighter with each step, its pulsations syncing with her racing heartbeat. She stepped through the threshold, her breath hitching as the room came into view.

The space was nothing like the rest of the cottage. The walls and ceiling seemed to dissolve into endless black, speckled with faint, shimmering points of light like distant stars. At the center of the room hovered a shimmering, unstable gateway. It twisted and rippled, its edges glowing faintly as though alive. The light it cast wasn't natural; it bent and refracted strangely, warping the room around it.

Sarah's eyes widened as she stepped closer, unable to look away. Through the rippling surface of the gateway, she could see glimpses of a world that defied everything she thought she knew. Towering structures spiraled impossibly upward, their forms constantly shifting as though caught between solid and liquid. Beings moved among them, their shapes flickering in and out of visibility. Some were humanoid, others utterly alien, their forms elongated and fluid. The landscape beyond was a riot of colors, hues she couldn't name bleeding together and flowing like rivers of light.

The air shimmered like heat waves on pavement, but instead of warmth, it exuded a bone-deep chill that made Sarah's hands tremble. Her skin prickled as though the very atoms of her body were being drawn toward the rift.

She took another step forward, her breath shallow. The hum of the gateway grew louder, vibrating through her chest. She couldn't tell if the sound came from outside or inside her own head.

"Liam?" she called, her voice barely audible over the low, resonant hum. Her words dissolved into the charged air, swallowed by the room.

The pull of the rift grew stronger as she approached, her body leaning toward it involuntarily. Every instinct screamed at her to stop, to turn back, but Liam's voice called to her again, soft and pleading.

"Sarah, please... It's beautiful here."

She stopped a few feet from the gateway, her hands clenched into fists at her sides. Tears pricked her eyes, a desperate mix of hope and fear rising in her chest. "Liam, where are you?" she whispered, her voice cracking.

The light within the rift pulsed brighter, momentarily blinding her. She raised a hand to shield her eyes, squinting against the glow. When the light dimmed, the figure of a boy appeared just beyond the threshold. He was faint, his outline shimmering like a mirage, but his face was unmistakable.

"Liam?" she said again, louder this time. Her feet moved forward, and she reached out instinctively.

But before she could cross the threshold, another sound erupted from the rift. It was deep and guttural, unlike anything she had ever heard. The air grew heavier, the vibrations from the sound rattling her bones. The figure of Liam flickered his face twisting into something unrecognizable before vanishing entirely.

Sarah stumbled back, her heart pounding as the sound grew louder. It was joined by another voice, alien and distorted, speaking in a language she couldn't understand. The light of the rift shifted, taking on a darker, more menacing hue. Shapes moved within it, their forms chaotic and incomprehensible.

"No," she whispered, shaking her head. "No, this isn't real."

The pull of the gateway became unbearable, dragging her toward it like an invisible tide. She dug her heels into the floor, her hands gripping the edges of a nearby table for support. The hum of the rift turned into a roar, filling her ears and drowning out her thoughts.

"Sarah..." Liam's voice called again, but it sounded wrong now, warped and distant.

The air around her grew colder, the bone-deep chill seeping into her core. Her breath came in short, frantic gasps as she fought against the pull. The shapes within the rift became clearer, their movements frantic and chaotic. One of them turned toward her, its form stretching and elongating as it reached for the threshold.

"Stop," she whispered, tears streaming down her face. "Just stop."

The shape recoiled, as though her words had reached it. The light within the rift pulsed violently, and the guttural voice let out a sound that could only be described as laughter. The room trembled, the walls vibrating with the force of it.

And then, with a deafening crack, the door behind her slammed shut.

The light from the rift dimmed instantly, plunging the room into near darkness. The hum faded, leaving behind an oppressive silence that made her ears ring. Sarah collapsed to the floor, her body trembling as she gasped for air. The coldness lingered, wrapping around her like a suffocating shroud.

She stared at the rift, its light now faint and pulsing weakly. The shapes within it had disappeared, leaving only the swirling, incomprehensible landscape beyond. Her mind raced, struggling to process what she had seen.

"It's not real," she whispered, her voice shaky. "It can't be real."

But deep down, she knew it was. The cottage had shown her something that shouldn't exist, something that defied every law of nature and reason. And it wasn't done with her yet.

CHAPTER 9: THE VISITOR'S ECHO

Sarah sat motionless in the armchair, her body shivering despite the oppressive heat that seemed to radiate from the walls. Her mind raced, replaying the impossible images she'd seen beyond the rift. She clutched the blanket draped over the armrest; her knuckles white as her nails dug into the fabric. The whispers had gone silent for the first time in what felt like hours, leaving her with only the sound of her own ragged breathing.

Then came the footsteps.

At first, they were faint, so soft she thought she'd imagined them. But as they grew louder, closer, the deliberate rhythm made the hair on her arms stand on end. Someone—or something—was moving through the cottage. Her heart thudded painfully in her chest as she glanced toward the hallway, expecting to see the door at the end creak open further.

But it didn't.

Instead, the footsteps stopped in the living room.

"Hello?" Sarah's voice was barely more than a whisper. The room's dim light flickered, and her breath caught as a figure began to materialize near the fireplace.

It was a man, though the edges of his form flickered and glitched as though he were an image projected onto broken glass. He wore clothes from another era—a heavy wool coat that looked too warm for the season, with a scarf draped loosely around his neck. His face was pale, his eyes sunken and haunted. He turned slowly, his gaze locking onto Sarah.

"It's hungry," he muttered, his voice distorted as though layered with static. "Don't let it in."

Sarah shot to her feet, her back pressing against the wall. Her throat felt tight, her words caught somewhere between disbelief and terror. The man didn't move toward her, his body trembling slightly as though he were struggling to remain upright.

"Who are you?" she managed to say, her voice shaking. "What is this place?"

The man's head twitched to the side, his movements jerky and unnatural. "It twists you," he said, his voice softer now, almost mournful. "Shows you what you want, but it's not real. It takes."

Sarah's stomach churned. "What does it take?"

The man's eyes darted toward the hallway, his form flickering violently. He opened his mouth to speak, but the words came out garbled, incomprehensible. He raised a trembling hand, pointing toward Sarah.

"You can't..." he began, his voice breaking. Then his form glitched again, his body dissolving into a haze of static and shadow. He reappeared a moment later, but he seemed weaker, fainter.

"What are you trying to tell me?" Sarah took a hesitant step forward, her desperation overriding her fear.

The man's gaze met hers, and for a brief moment, his form stabilized. His eyes, filled with pain and urgency, bore into hers.

"Leave," he said, his voice barely audible. "Before it's too late."

Sarah opened her mouth to ask more questions, but before she could speak, the man let out a strangled cry. His body convulsed, his image flickering faster and faster until he collapsed to his knees. A low, guttural sound echoed through the room, vibrating the air around her.

The man's head snapped up, his eyes wide with terror. "It knows," he said, his voice breaking. "It knows you're here."

And then he was gone. His body dissolved into mist, the faint static that had surrounded him dissipating into the air. Sarah stood frozen, her chest heaving as her mind raced to process what had just happened.

She lowered her gaze to the floor where the man had been. Something gleamed faintly in the dim light. She crouched down, her trembling hands closing around a small object. It was a key, old and tarnished, with symbols etched into its surface. Her stomach twisted as she realized the carvings matched the ones on the locked door.

The whispers began again, louder this time, their tone urgent and accusing. Sarah's hands tightened around the key, her pulse pounding in her ears. She stood slowly, her legs unsteady beneath her. The cottage seemed to shift around her, the walls pressing closer as though alive.

"What do you want from me?" she shouted, her voice cracking. The whispers didn't answer, but their intensity grew, filling her mind with fragments of words she couldn't piece together.

Her gaze drifted toward the hallway, where the locked door waited. The air seemed colder now, the light dimmer. She clutched the key tightly, its metal biting into her palm. The man's final words echoed in her mind.

It knows you're here.

Despite the terror that gripped her, a flicker of determination ignited in her chest. She didn't know what the cottage wanted or why it had brought her here, but she knew she couldn't leave without understanding the truth.

With trembling hands, she turned toward the hallway, the key heavy in her grasp. The whispers followed her, growing louder with each step.

CHAPTER 10: MANIFESTATIONS

Sarah stirred awake, the haze of sleep retreating as the faint smell of freshly brewed coffee reached her nose. For a moment, she thought she was home. The soft clatter of dishes and the faint hum of a familiar tune filled the air. She blinked groggily, her eyes adjusting to the golden light spilling into the room.

She froze.

Liam was sitting at the dining table.

Her heart stopped as she took in the sight. He looked just as she remembered: tousled hair, the faintest smirk playing on his lips as he stirred his coffee. He glanced up and grinned.

"Morning, sleepyhead," he said casually, as though nothing had ever happened. "Took you long enough to wake up. I've been waiting."

Sarah's breath caught. "Liam?" she whispered, her voice trembling.

He raised an eyebrow. "Who else?" He gestured to the chair opposite him. "Sit. You must be starving."

Her legs moved on autopilot, carrying her to the table. She lowered herself into the chair, her eyes locked on him. He looked so real—every detail perfect, down to the small scar above his eyebrow from when he fell off his bike as a kid. Her chest tightened, a knot of grief and hope tangling inside her.

"You found it, Sarah," Liam said, his voice warm and steady. "I knew you would."

For a moment, she let herself believe it. She reached for the coffee he slid toward her, her hands trembling as she wrapped her fingers around the warm mug. The aroma was rich and familiar, grounding her in a reality she desperately wanted to accept.

"How...?" she began, her voice breaking. "How are you here?"

Liam shrugged, leaning back in his chair. "Does it matter? I'm here. You're here. That's what counts."

Her eyes filled with tears as she reached across the table, her fingers brushing against his hand. He felt solid, warm. Real. The knot in her chest loosened just enough to let a sob escape her lips.

"I missed you," she said, her voice cracking. "I thought I'd lost you forever."

He smiled, but something in his expression flickered—a subtle shift that made her pull her hand back. His grin seemed too wide now, his teeth too perfect, too uniform. She blinked, trying to shake off the feeling.

As the moments stretched, the cracks began to show.

Liam's voice carried a strange undertone, like a faint static buzzing beneath his words. His movements became less fluid, more deliberate. And his eyes... they didn't quite meet hers anymore. They hovered just off-center, as though he were looking through her rather than at her.

"How did you find it?" he asked, his tone light but his smile frozen in place. "The cottage. Tell me."

Sarah's chest tightened. "Liam, what..." She trailed off, her voice trembling. "What's going on?"

"What do you mean?" he said, his grin widening. "I'm here, Sarah.

Isn't this what you wanted?"

Her stomach churned as the static in his voice grew louder, the edges of his form flickering subtly. She pushed her chair back, her instincts screaming that something was wrong.

"You're not him," she said, her voice shaking. "You're not Liam."

The illusion faltered. His smile froze, his eyes darkening as his head tilted at an unnatural angle.

"Don't do this," he said, his voice layered with static. "You wanted this. You came here for me."

Sarah's breaths came in short, shallow gasps. "You're not real," she said, louder this time. "You're not him."

The illusion shattered.

Liam's form dissolved into shadow, the room around her distorting as though the walls themselves were bending. The table collapsed into itself, the coffee spilling upward, defying gravity as it evaporated into the air. Sarah stumbled back, her hands clutching at the edges of the chair for support.

The cottage struck back.

The walls began to bleed, dark rivulets streaming down in unnatural patterns. The whispers returned, louder than ever, turning into guttural screams that filled the air. The floor beneath her tilted violently, sending her sprawling onto the ground. She scrambled to her feet, her heart pounding as the room seemed to spin around her.

"Stop!" she screamed, her voice drowned out by the chaos. "What do you want from me?"

The walls pulsed, the shadows stretching toward her like living things. The air grew colder, every breath she took burning her lungs. She backed away, her hands searching for anything solid to hold onto.

The whispers reached a deafening crescendo, their unintelligible words pressing into her mind like jagged shards of glass. The room tilted again, the floor splintering beneath her feet. She let out a choked sob as she stumbled toward the doorway, her only thought to escape.

She burst into the next room, slamming the door shut behind her. The air was eerily still, the silence pressing against her ears like a physical weight. She collapsed to the floor, her chest heaving as she tried to catch her breath. Her hands trembled as she ran them through her hair, her mind racing.

The cottage wasn't done with her. She knew that now. It was playing with her, twisting her grief and fear into weapons. But she couldn't let it break her.

She wouldn't.

As the silence stretched, Sarah forced herself to stand. Her legs wobbled beneath her, but she steadied herself against the wall. She couldn't let it win. Not now. Not ever.

CHAPTER 11: THE RIFT EXPANDS

The silence didn't last. It was never truly silent in the cottage. Sarah leaned against the wall, her breathing uneven, her pulse thrumming in her ears. The air was wrong here. It felt heavier, thicker, as though it carried something alive within it. She pressed her palms to her temples, willing the nausea to pass.

Then she saw it: a ripple in the wall across from her.

Her breath caught as she stepped closer, her eyes fixed on the distortion. The wallpaper bulged slightly, pulsating in rhythm with some unseen force. Her fingers hovered over the surface, and the moment her skin made contact, the wall shuddered beneath her touch. A low hum filled the room, resonating deep in her chest.

She stumbled back, her heart pounding. "No," she whispered. "No, not again."

The hum grew louder, and with it, the wall began to crack. Tiny fissures spiderwebbed outward, their edges glowing faintly. Something pushed through the breaks—tendrils, glassy and delicate, yet moving with an unnerving purpose. They writhed as though tasting the air, emitting a faint, melodic hum that was almost soothing. Almost.

Sarah pressed herself against the opposite wall, her chest heaving. "What is this?" she whispered, her voice trembling. The tendrils continued to grow, snaking down the wall and pooling on the floor. They looked alien, their surfaces shimmering with shifting colors that defied description.

The floor beneath her feet began to creak. She glanced down, her stomach twisting as she noticed similar cracks forming at her feet. More tendrils emerged, weaving their way upward, brushing against her boots.

Panic surged through her, and she bolted for the hallway. But before she reached the door, a sudden flash of light stopped her in her tracks. A new doorway appeared in the center of the living room, materializing out of thin air. It shimmered, its edges jagged and unstable, pulsing with the same otherworldly energy as the tendrils. The hum became a roar, filling the entire space.

Sarah froze, her mind screaming for her to run, but her body refused to move. Through the doorway, she could see it: the alien dimension. The world beyond was unlike anything she'd ever imagined. Towering spires twisted upward into a sky that pulsed with shifting colors. The ground rippled like liquid, and strange, flickering shapes moved in the distance, their forms constantly shifting and reforming.

Her stomach churned as she stared into the impossible landscape. It was beautiful in a way that made her feel small and insignificant, a speck in the vast expanse of something far greater than she could comprehend.

Then it stepped through.

The creature was humanoid, but only barely. Its body flickered like a faulty hologram, its edges blurred and inconsistent. It moved with an unsettling grace, its elongated limbs flowing unnaturally as though not entirely bound by this reality. Its face—if it could be called that—was featureless, a smooth surface that shimmered faintly.

Sarah's breath hitched as the creature stopped just inside the doorway. It turned toward her, or at least she thought it did. There were no eyes to meet, no expression to read, but she felt its attention on her. A cold wave washed over her, rooting her in place.

"What do you want?" she whispered, her voice barely audible.

The creature didn't respond. It took a slow, deliberate step closer, its movements hypnotic. The air around it seemed to warp, the tendrils on the floor recoiling as though in deference to its presence. Sarah's instincts screamed at her to run, but her body wouldn't obey.

Then it reached out.

The creature's hand—if it could be called that—brushed against her arm. Its touch was cold, sending a jolt through her body. Her vision blurred, and for a moment, the world around her shifted. She was no longer in the cottage but standing in the alien landscape she'd glimpsed through the rift. The air was thin and sharp, the colors around her too vibrant, almost painful to look at.

A voice echoed in her mind, not words but sensations. Fear. Curiosity. Hunger.

Then she was back in the cottage, gasping for air. She stumbled backward, clutching her arm where the creature had touched her. A faint, glowing mark pulsed on her skin, its intricate lines resembling the symbols she'd seen carved into the walls and the notebook. It felt warm, almost alive, and with it came a sensation she couldn't shake—a connection to the alien dimension, as though it were calling her home.

"No," she said, her voice trembling. "I'm not... I'm not yours."

The creature tilted its head, as if considering her words. Then, without warning, it stepped back through the doorway, its form dissolving into the rippling light. The doorway itself began to collapse, the edges folding inward until it disappeared completely.

Sarah sank to the floor, her body trembling. The room was silent again, but the mark on her arm continued to pulse faintly, a constant reminder of what had just happened. She clutched it tightly, her mind racing with questions she couldn't begin to answer.

The cottage had shown her many things, but this... this was something else entirely. It wasn't just alive. It wasn't just feeding on her fears. It was connected to something far bigger, far more terrifying than she'd ever imagined.

CHAPTER 12: THE RIFT'S HISTORY

The glow of the mark on Sarah's arm dimmed as the tremors in her body subsided. She sat cross-legged on the floor, her back against the cold wall, staring at the journal in her lap. Its cracked leather cover felt heavier now, as though the knowledge it contained had taken on physical weight. She flipped through the pages again, her fingers trembling as they skimmed the chaotic scrawls and jagged symbols that lined the brittle paper.

The cottage isn't a place.

That phrase appeared over and over, sometimes underlined, sometimes scrawled in large, frantic letters across entire pages. Sarah paused on a section where the handwriting changed, becoming smaller, neater—almost reverent:

It is a bridge, not meant for us, but we are drawn to it. Some are chosen, sifted, filtered… the rest are consumed.

Her stomach churned as she read the words again. The word *consumed* felt like it had been scratched into her skin, its meaning more visceral with every passing second. The next paragraph was fragmented, as though the writer had been interrupted mid-thought:

The light isn't salvation. The rift… a door that hungers… not—

The sentence ended there; the ink smudged as though the writer's hand had been dragged across the page. Sarah's mind raced. She couldn't shake the memory of the creature, its touch, and the alien voice that had wormed its way into her thoughts. It wasn't just the cottage. The entire dimension was alive.

She turned another page, her breath catching as she found a rough sketch of the symbols carved into the walls. Each one was drawn with painstaking detail, their lines sharp and deliberate. Beneath the drawing was a single line of text:

They are not decorations. They are warnings.

Sarah traced the lines with her fingertip, her pulse quickening. Warnings. Her gaze drifted to the walls around her. The symbols were faint, barely visible beneath the peeling wallpaper, but they were there. She'd seen them before, though she hadn't understood their purpose.

Another note, scrawled in a different hand, was squeezed into the margin:

Do not trust the light. Resist the pull.

Her fingers brushed the glowing mark on her arm, and a wave of unease washed over her. It wasn't just a connection. It was a tether, a way for the rift to reel her in when it was ready. The thought made her skin crawl.

The air shifted suddenly, growing colder. The hum of the cottage grew louder, resonating in her bones. Her head snapped up as the room darkened, the light from the windows dimming until it was almost nonexistent. The journal fell from her lap as her vision blurred, her surroundings melting into shadow.

A flash of light erupted before her, and with it came a vision.

She was no longer in the cottage. The walls dissolved into darkness, replaced by an infinite void. In the center of it stood a man. He wore clothes that looked decades, maybe centuries old: a dark waistcoat and a high-collared shirt stained with sweat and blood. His face was pale, his features sharp with exhaustion, but his eyes burned with determination.

The man stood before the rift. It was smaller then, more unstable, its edges flickering violently. He held a small object in his hand—a pendant, or maybe a key—its surface etched with the same symbols that lined the cottage walls. He spoke, though Sarah couldn't hear the words. His voice was drowned out by the roar of the rift, the sound like tearing metal.

The man's movements were frantic. He pressed the object against the edge of the rift, his body shaking with effort. The light around him grew brighter, almost blinding, and Sarah's heart clenched as she realized what was happening. He was sacrificing himself.

The rift shrank, its edges folding inward as the man's form dissolved into the light. His scream pierced the void, a sound of pain and resolve that sent a shiver down Sarah's spine. And then, silence.

Sarah gasped as the vision ended, her body jerking violently as she was thrust back into the present. She was on her hands and knees, the journal splayed open in front of her. Her breathing was ragged, her heart pounding so hard it felt like it might break free of her chest.

"What was that?" she whispered, her voice barely audible.

The cottage didn't answer, but the hum in the walls felt heavier now, more deliberate. She glanced at the journal, her eyes landing on a final note scribbled hastily at the bottom of the page:

He is part of it now. We all are.

The realization hit her like a physical blow. The cottage's sentience wasn't just its own. It was made up of the people it had taken, their essence woven into its walls, its floors, its very being. Every creak, every whisper—they weren't just echoes of the past. They were alive.

Sarah's hands trembled as she picked up the journal and clutched it tightly to her chest. She needed to find a way to stop it. To end this. But how could she fight something so vast, so ancient, so deeply rooted in the fabric of reality?

The glowing mark on her arm pulsed faintly, as though in response to her thoughts. She looked down at it, her jaw tightening. Whatever this connection was, it wasn't going to let her go without a fight. But neither was she.

"You won't take me," she said through gritted teeth, her voice steady despite the fear coursing through her. "You won't win."

The cottage seemed to rumble in response, the hum rising to a low, guttural growl. But Sarah didn't flinch. She stood, her resolve hardening as she stepped toward the hallway. She didn't know how this would end, but one thing was certain:

She wasn't going to let it consume her.

CHAPTER 13: THE KEEPER

The hum in the walls seemed to deepen as Sarah stepped into the main room. Her breath came in uneven bursts, her legs trembling beneath her. She clutched the journal tightly against her chest, her gaze darting around the room for signs of movement. The cottage felt different now, more oppressive. The air was thick, heavy with the sense of being watched.

Then it happened.

The shadows at the edge of the room coalesced, pooling together like spilled ink. They shifted and writhed, forming a shape that was both familiar and alien. The figure that emerged stood tall and still, its form flickering like a projection struggling to remain stable. It was neither fully human nor fully alien—its features shifting constantly, as though it couldn't decide what to be.

"Sarah," the figure said, its voice low and resonant, layered with tones both human and otherworldly. The sound vibrated in her chest, making her heart skip a beat. "You were chosen."

Her grip on the journal tightened, her knuckles white. "Who are you?" she demanded, her voice steadier than she felt. "What do you want?"

The figure tilted its head, its shifting face almost resembling a smile. "I am the Keeper," it said. "I am the will of the gateway. The bridge."

"The cottage," Sarah whispered, the words tasting bitter on her tongue.

The Keeper nodded. "It saw your pain, your potential. That is why you are here."

Sarah's chest tightened. "You mean... it brought me here? For what? To consume me like the others?"

The Keeper's form flickered, its voice calm but insistent. "You misunderstand. The gateway does not destroy. It transforms. It offers freedom from the chains of your humanity—freedom from grief, from guilt, from fear."

"Freedom?" Sarah's voice cracked, her anger rising. "You mean obliteration. Losing everything that makes me *me*."

The Keeper took a step closer, and Sarah instinctively backed away. Its presence was overwhelming, the air around it warping and vibrating. "You cling to an identity forged by suffering. Why endure such pain when you can become something more? Something infinite."

"No," Sarah said firmly, her voice shaking. "I won't let you... twist me into whatever *that*"—she gestured toward the glowing mark on her arm—"is supposed to be."

The Keeper's head tilted again, its shifting face betraying no emotion. "You resist, but the gateway is patient. It feeds on resistance as much as acceptance. Either way, it will take what it needs."

Sarah's mind raced. Every instinct screamed at her to run, but she couldn't tear her gaze away from the Keeper. "Why me?" she asked, her voice quieter now. "Why not someone else?"

The Keeper's form seemed to stabilize briefly, its voice softening. "The gateway sees what lies within. Your grief... your guilt. You carry the weight of your brother's death as though it were your own. You ache to make sense of it, to find a purpose in his absence. The gateway offers that purpose."

Tears burned at the corners of Sarah's eyes. "You don't know me," she said through gritted teeth. "You don't know anything about me."

"Don't I?" the Keeper asked, its voice low and haunting. "The journal you clutch so tightly—you think it holds answers. But it only reflects your fears, your doubts. The truth is already within you."

Sarah shook her head, her nails digging into the journal's cover. "No. You're lying."

The Keeper took another step forward, its form towering over her now. "Resisting the gateway has consequences. It will not let you go without a price. You can fight, but it will consume you piece by piece until there is nothing left."

"Then I'll fight," Sarah snapped, her voice firm despite the tears streaming down her face. "I'll fight with everything I have."

The Keeper paused, its flickering form growing dimmer. "We shall see," it said, its tone laced with quiet menace.

Without another word, the Keeper dissolved into shadow, its presence evaporating as though it had never been there. The room fell silent, the hum of the walls fading to an almost imperceptible vibration.

Sarah stood alone, her chest heaving, the journal still clutched tightly in her arms. The mark on her arm pulsed faintly, a constant reminder of the gateway's pull. She didn't know how to stop it, but one thing was certain:

She wasn't giving in.

CHAPTER 14: THE COTTAGE TIGHTENS ITS GRIP

The walls groaned as though alive, their timbre low and resonant, vibrating in Sarah's chest. The air in the cottage had thickened, carrying an unshakable sense of dread. She turned a corner, her footsteps muffled by the shifting wood beneath her, and froze.

The hallway stretched infinitely ahead, its flickering sconces lighting a path that defied reason. Her pulse quickened as she spun around, expecting to see the room she'd just left. Instead, she found another endless corridor behind her, identical to the one in front.

"No," she whispered, gripping the journal tightly. Her palms were damp, the worn leather slipping slightly in her grasp. "This isn't real."

She began walking, her breaths shallow. Each step echoed unnaturally, as though the sound were being distorted and thrown back at her from all directions. Doors lined the walls, some slightly ajar, others sealed shut. She reached for the nearest one and hesitated, her hand trembling over the brass knob.

You have to keep moving, she thought, swallowing the lump in her throat. She turned the handle and pushed.

The door opened not into another room but into an expanse of stars. Sarah stumbled back, her breath hitching. The floor dropped away, leaving nothing but an infinite void stretching in all directions. Floating islands of shimmering light drifted lazily in the distance, their surfaces reflecting impossible landscapes. One looked like her childhood backyard, another like the alien dimension beyond the rift.

"No," she muttered again, slamming the door shut. Her heart pounded as she turned and ran, the walls seeming to close in around her. She yanked open another door, and this time she found herself in a room that was eerily familiar.

Her childhood bedroom.

Everything was exactly as she remembered: the faded posters on the walls, the worn-out comforter draped over her bed, the cluttered desk covered in doodles and scraps of paper. But the air was thick with tension, the shadows in the corners too dark, too alive.

"Sarah," a voice called softly.

She spun around, her chest tightening. Sitting on the edge of the bed was Liam. He looked exactly as he had the last time she'd seen him—disheveled hair, a crooked smile that didn't quite reach his eyes.

"Liam?" she whispered, her voice breaking. Her feet felt rooted to the floor, her body frozen between reaching for him and running away.

He tilted his head, his expression twisting into something she didn't recognize. "You didn't save me."

Her heart shattered at the words. "I… I tried," she stammered, tears streaming down her face. "I didn't know how to…"

Liam stood, his movements unnatural, jerky. His eyes darkened, his smile stretching too wide. "You left me. You let me die."

"No," Sarah cried, shaking her head. "That's not true. I—"

"You didn't even try," he hissed, his voice growing louder, more distorted. "You were too scared. Too weak."

The room began to warp, the walls bending inward, the floor tilting beneath her. Liam's form flickered, his face twisting into something monstrous. "You can't save anyone," he said, his voice overlapping with a dozen others. "Not even yourself."

Sarah's knees buckled, and she clutched her head, her thoughts a whirlwind of guilt and denial. The shadows in the room surged toward her, clawing at her mind. But somewhere deep inside, a spark of defiance flared.

"You're not real," she whispered, her voice trembling but growing stronger. "This isn't real."

The shadows hesitated, their edges rippling. Sarah forced herself to her feet, her fists clenched. "You're not Liam. You're just another lie."

The figure snarled, its voice rising to a deafening scream. "You'll never escape. You'll never be free."

Sarah took a step forward, her heart pounding but her resolve was unshaken. "I don't care what you are. You won't control me."

The room shattered like glass, the fragments dissolving into darkness. Sarah stumbled, her breath coming in ragged gasps as the world around her reformed. She was back in the central hallway, the journal still clutched tightly to her chest.

The locked door stood before her; its surface etched with glowing symbols. But it was no longer locked. The door hung wide open, the darkness beyond it pulsing with an otherworldly light. The hum in the walls grew louder, resonating with the beat of her heart.

Sarah wiped her face, her tears mixing with the sweat on her skin. She squared her shoulders, her fear still present but no longer in control.

"Let's finish this," she said, stepping toward the door.

CHAPTER 15: THE DOOR BEYOND REALITY

The hum of the walls grew louder as Sarah stepped closer to the glowing doorway. It pulsed with a rhythm that resonated deep within her chest, as though the very air around her was alive. She paused at the threshold, her hand hovering just inches from the doorframe. The symbols etched into the surface glowed faintly, their light shifting like liquid gold.

Her breath hitched. "If I go in," she whispered, her voice trembling, "there's no turning back. But staying here…" She glanced behind her at the darkened hallway, the suffocating presence of the cottage pressing closer. "Staying here isn't safe either."

She closed her eyes, took a deep breath, and stepped through.

The world on the other side swallowed her whole.

The air shifted instantly, sharp and electric against her skin. The ground beneath her feet was solid but translucent, a surface of rippling light that shimmered with every step she took. Above her, the sky stretched endlessly, a kaleidoscope of shifting colors that bled into one another, forming patterns that hurt to look at for too long. Floating islands spiraled lazily through the air, their surfaces dotted with glowing plants that pulsed like living things.

Sarah's chest tightened as she took in the impossible beauty of the alien dimension. "It's… beautiful," she whispered. "Horrible. Both at once."

Her senses struggled to process the landscape. Sounds hummed at the edges of her hearing, a symphony of faint whispers and melodic tones that seemed to come from everywhere and nowhere at once. The air carried a metallic tang, sharp and unnatural, but not entirely unpleasant.

She took a cautious step forward, her boots sinking slightly into the rippling surface. The ground seemed to respond to her presence, shifting and reshaping itself as though alive. A cold chill ran down her spine as she glanced at her arm. The glowing mark left by the creature in the cottage pulsed faintly, its light mirroring the rhythm of the world around her.

"What is this place?" she muttered, her voice swallowed by the vastness of the dimension.

The sky above her shifted, a ripple of shadow passing through the colors like a storm cloud. Her skin tingled, and her heartbeat slowed unnaturally, each thud echoing in her ears. She stumbled, her breath catching as her thoughts began to fracture. Faint echoes of her own voice whispered at the edges of her mind, repeating words she didn't recognize.

You belong here.

Let go.

Become.

Sarah shook her head violently, her hands flying to her ears as though that could block out the invasive whispers. "No," she said through gritted teeth. "You won't take me."

The ground beneath her trembled, sending ripples of light cascading outward. In the distance, a shadowy figure emerged, its form flickering like a mirage. Sarah's breath caught as the figure moved closer, its gait slow but deliberate. Her chest tightened, and she clenched her fists, steeling herself.

"Who's there?" she called, her voice steady despite the fear curling in her stomach.

The figure didn't answer. It drew closer, its form becoming clearer with each step. It was tall and humanoid, but its edges wavered as though it weren't fully in this reality. Its body was covered in dark, shimmering patterns that seemed to shift and flow like liquid metal.

Sarah's pulse quickened as the figure stopped a few feet away. Its face was obscured, its features shifting constantly, making it impossible to discern any specific details. The air around it felt heavier, charged with energy that made her skin crawl.

"You," the figure said, its voice low and layered with tones both human and alien. "You have crossed the threshold."

"Who are you?" Sarah demanded; her voice was firmer than she felt. "What do you want?"

The figure tilted its head, its form flickering. "I am a fragment," it said cryptically. "A piece of what came before. And you... you are the next."

Sarah's chest tightened. "The next what?"

The figure didn't answer. Instead, it raised a hand, pointing toward her. The glowing mark on her arm flared brightly, sending a jolt of searing pain through her body. She cried out, falling to her knees as the world around her blurred.

Images flooded her mind—fragments of memories that weren't her own. She saw people stepping through the rift, their faces filled with awe and terror. She saw the dimension consuming them, reshaping their bodies and minds into something unrecognizable. She saw the cottage, standing as a bridge between the worlds, its walls alive with the whispers of those it had taken.

And then she saw herself.

She was standing in the center of the dimension, her body flickering like the figure before her. Her eyes glowed with an unnatural light, and her voice… it was not her own.

You cannot fight forever, the voice in her mind said. *You will become.*

The vision shattered, and Sarah gasped, the pain in her arm subsided. She looked up to find the figure still standing before her, its head tilted as though observing her.

"You see now," it said, its voice softer. "This is what waits. This is what you were chosen for."

Sarah staggered to her feet, her legs trembling but her resolve unshaken. "I don't care what you think I'm here for," she said, her voice steady. "I'm not going to let this place take me."

The figure paused, its form flickering again. "We shall see," it said, before dissolving into the air, leaving Sarah alone once more.

The dimension around her pulsed, the colors growing brighter and more erratic. The ground beneath her feet shifted, and she stumbled forward, her breath coming in short gasps. She didn't know how long she could hold on, but one thing was certain:

She had to find a way out.

CHAPTER 16: THE KEEPER'S TRUTH

The dimension pulsed with an otherworldly rhythm, the rippling ground beneath Sarah's feet shifting with each step she took. The shimmering sky above her bled with colors that defied logic, hues she could see but not name. The air was sharp and cold, tasting of metal and static. Every breath she drew felt heavier, as though the atmosphere itself resisted her presence.

Then the Keeper appeared.

Its form emerged from the rippling horizon, flickering between solid and translucent like a shadow caught in a broken projector. In this realm, the Keeper looked less human, its shifting features alien and undefined. Its body elongated unnaturally, tendrils of dark energy trailing behind it. Its presence was immense, the weight of it pressing down on Sarah like a physical force.

"You've come farther than most," the Keeper said, its voice resonating in her chest. It spoke not with words but with an amalgamation of the sound and sensation that Sarah felt more than she heard. "That is a testament to your will… and your pain."

Sarah clenched her fists, forcing herself to stand tall. "What do you want from me?" she demanded, her voice trembling but defiant.

The Keeper tilted its head, its form shifting and flickering. "Want?" it echoed. "I am not here to want. I am here to guide. To offer."

"Offer what?" Sarah's voice was sharp, laced with anger. "More lies? More manipulation?"

The Keeper's form stilled, its gaze—if it could be called that—fixing on her. "Truth," it said simply.

The Keeper gestured to the dimension around them, its tendrils flowing like smoke. "This place," it began, "is not a prison, as you believe. It is a sanctuary. A realm of purity where fear, regret, and identity dissolve. Here, beings transcend the limits of flesh and mind."

Sarah shook her head, her heart pounding. "You call this purity?" she said, gesturing to the chaotic, alien landscape. "It's madness. Nothing here makes sense."

"To you," the Keeper replied, its voice calm, almost soothing. "You cling to the constructs of your world—time, form, individuality. But those are chains, Sarah. Chains that bind you to pain."

"Pain is part of life," Sarah snapped. "It's what makes us human."

The Keeper's form flickered, its tendrils coiling like restless serpents. "And what has your humanity brought you? Grief. Guilt. Suffering. You carry so much weight, Sarah. All of it could be erased."

Sarah's chest tightened. The glowing mark on her arm pulsed faintly, a constant reminder of the connection she couldn't sever. "If I give that up," she said, her voice quieter now, "what's left of me?"

The Keeper stepped closer, its presence towering over her. "Freedom," it said. "Freedom from the burden of memory. From the ache of loss. You would become something greater, something infinite."

Sarah's mind raced, her thoughts a whirlwind of doubt

and defiance. She thought of Liam, his laugh, his stubborn determination. She thought of the moments they had shared, the fights, the laughter, the love. Could she truly let all of that go? Could she erase the pain of his loss without losing the memory of him entirely?

"No," she said firmly, meeting the Keeper's gaze. "I won't do it. I won't give up who I am."

The Keeper's tendrils stilled, its form shifting closer. "Resist all you want," it said, its voice carrying a faint edge of amusement. "This place will wear you down. The gateway's pull is inexorable. You will see, in time."

It extended a hand, its dark, flickering fingers reaching toward her. "But why delay the inevitable?" it asked. "Take the next step. Shed your pain. Embrace what lies beyond."

Sarah stared at the outstretched hand, her pulse roaring in her ears. The air around her felt heavier, charged with the weight of the Keeper's presence. She could feel the dimension pressing against her mind, its whispers growing louder, more insistent.

But she shook her head, stepping back. "You can't have me," she said, her voice steady despite the fear clawing at her chest. "I'll fight you until the end."

The Keeper tilted its head, its form flickering as it withdrew its hand. "So be it," it said. "But know this, Sarah: the longer you resist, the harder it will become. This place will test you. It will break you. And when it does, I will be here to pick up the pieces."

The air shimmered, and the Keeper's form began to dissolve, its tendrils unraveling into the swirling light of the dimension. "You cannot fight forever," it said, its voice echoing as it vanished. "No one ever does."

Sarah stood alone, her chest heaving as the dimension around her seemed to ripple in response to her emotions. The mark on her arm flared brightly, sending a wave of heat through her body. She clutched it tightly, her nails digging into her skin.

"I'll find a way," she muttered, her voice fierce. "I'll find a way to end this."

The dimension pulsed, the colors above her darkening slightly. The Keeper's warning echoed in her mind, but she refused to let it take hold. She had come this far. She wasn't giving up now.

Steeling herself, Sarah took a step forward, deeper into the alien realm.

CHAPTER 17: THE DIMENSION'S TESTS

The alien dimension seemed to pulse with awareness, its shimmering landscapes shifting as Sarah moved deeper into the realm. The ground beneath her feet rippled like liquid glass, reflecting the swirling, impossible sky above. Each step felt heavier, as though the air itself resisted her defiance. She pressed a hand to the glowing mark on her arm, its heat a constant reminder of the tether binding her to this place.

Then the world shifted.

Without warning, the horizon folded inward, colors bleeding together until they reformed into a new scene. Sarah blinked, disoriented, as she found herself standing in a familiar setting: her childhood home. The cozy living room was unchanged, down to the worn armchair by the window and the faint smell of her mother's lavender air freshener.

"No," she whispered, her heart sinking. "This isn't real."

But the sound of footsteps made her whirl around. Standing in the doorway was Liam, alive and whole. His face was lit with a smile that didn't quite reach his eyes, and his voice was soft as he spoke.

"Sarah," he said, stepping closer. "You found me."

Her chest tightened, tears welling up as she struggled to keep her resolve. "You're not him," she said, her voice trembling. "You're just another trick."

Liam's expression faltered, his brow furrowing. "Why do you always push me away?" he asked, his tone tinged with hurt. "You could have saved me, Sarah. You knew how much I needed you."

"Stop it," she said, backing away. Her hands shook as she clenched them into fists. "You're not real."

"You left me," he said, his voice growing louder, sharper. "You let me die because you were too scared. Too weak."

The room began to warp, the walls bending inward as Liam's form distorted. His face twisted, his eyes darkening as his smile stretched unnaturally wide. "You didn't even try to save me," he hissed, his voice overlapping with others, a cacophony of accusations.

Sarah's knees buckled, the weight of his words pressing down on her. The shadows in the room surged toward her, clawing at her mind with memories of guilt and regret.

"You're not taking this from me!" she screamed, her voice breaking. She pushed herself to her feet, her body trembling with effort. "You're not him. You're not real."

The shadows hesitated, their movements faltering. Sarah's anger burned through her fear as she took a step forward. "You can't use him against me," she said, her voice steady now. "I know who I am. I know what's real."

The illusion shattered like glass, fragments of the scene dissolved into the air. Sarah fell to her knees, gasping for breath. Her body felt weaker, as though the test had drained some vital parts of her. She glanced at the mark on her arm and saw that it had spread, thin lines of glowing light branching out like veins beneath her skin.

The dimension shifted again, the swirling sky folding in on itself before reforming into a new reality. Sarah blinked, her breath catching as she saw what lay before her.

She was standing in a spacious studio, sunlight streaming through tall windows. Canvases lined the walls, each one a masterpiece of color and emotion. A table in the center of the room held a collection of awards and photographs. One showed her smiling alongside a team of artists, another captured her standing on a stage, holding a trophy.

It was everything she'd ever dreamed of.

Her legs felt heavy as she stepped closer, her fingers brushing against one of the paintings. The texture was real, the smell of paint sharp in the air. A sense of peace settled over her, warm and inviting.

This is what you wanted; a voice whispered in her mind. *A life of success. A life without pain.*

She closed her eyes, her heart aching with longing. For a moment, she let herself imagine what it would be like to stay here, to leave behind the grief and fear that had haunted her for so long. But the warmth was fleeting, and the edges of the scene began to blur, cracks forming in the perfect illusion.

"It's not real," she said, her voice barely audible. Her hands clenched into fists as she repeated the words, louder this time. "It's not real!"

The studio trembled, the walls collapsing inward as the illusion dissolved. Sarah stumbled; her body wracked with exhaustion. The mark on her arm burned brighter, the veins of light spreading farther, reaching toward her shoulder.

She fell to her knees, her breath ragged. The ground beneath her pulsed, the dimension shifting around her like a living thing. She could feel it testing her, pushing her to the brink. Each trial left her weaker, more vulnerable to the pull of the alien realm.

But she wasn't done yet.

She forced herself to stand, her legs shaking beneath her. The swirling colors of the dimension darkened a storm brewing in the distance. Sarah took a deep breath, her resolve hardening as she stepped forward, deeper into the unknown.

The tests weren't over. She could feel the weight of another challenge looming ahead, but she refused to back down. Whatever the dimension threw at her next, she would face it.

She had no choice.

CHAPTER 18: THE GATEWAY'S PULL

The air grew thicker as Sarah trudged forward, the alien dimension tightening its grip with each step she took. Her legs felt heavy, her breaths shallow as though the atmosphere itself resisted her presence. The storm she'd seen in the distance churned closer, its swirling colors dark and foreboding, flashing with bursts of light that illuminated the impossible landscapes around her. Still, she pressed on, her resolve hardening even as her body screamed for rest.

At last, she saw it.

The rift.

It dominated the horizon, a vast, glowing tear in reality that pulsed with an otherworldly rhythm. Its edges shimmered like heat waves, distorting everything around it. Shapes floated within the rift, their forms shifting and twisting—some humanoid, others grotesque and alien. Faces flickered briefly before dissolving into formless masses, their mouths opening in silent screams.

Sarah's breath hitched as she stepped closer, the ground beneath her feet rippling with each movement. The mark on her arm burned, the veins of light spreading further across her skin. The pull of the rift was almost physical now, a magnetic force that tugged at her very being.

"The rift," she whispered, her voice swallowed by the hum that filled the air. "It's alive."

She stopped a few feet from the rift's edge, her heart pounding as she stared into its depths. The shapes inside moved with an eerie grace, their forms merging and separating in a chaotic dance. For a moment, she thought she saw Liam's face among them, his eyes wide with fear before his features dissolved into the swirling mass.

"No," she said, shaking her head. "You're not real. None of this is real."

But then it spoke.

The voice of the rift wasn't a single sound but a cacophony of whispers and echoes, each one overlapping and intertwining. It filled her mind, resonating deep within her chest.

"We can take it away," the voices said. "All of it. Just one step."

Sarah's knees buckled, and she fell to the ground, her hands clutching at her head. The whispers grew louder, drowning out her thoughts.

"No more pain," the voices continued. "No more fear. No more loss."

She clenched her teeth, forcing herself to speak. "What happens if I step through?"

The voices shifted, their tone almost soothing. "You become. You transcend. You are free."

As the words echoed in her mind, the rift shifted, and a vision formed within its swirling depths. Sarah saw herself stepping through the rift, her body dissolving into light as she merged with the dimension. The pain in her chest, the weight of her grief, all of it vanished. She floated among the other shapes, her form unrecognizable but at peace.

But then the vision twisted. She saw her memories unraveling, her identity dissolving until there was nothing left of the person she once was. Her laughter, her tears, her love for Liam—all of it consumed by the rift.

"Is it worth it?" she whispered, tears streaming down her face. "To lose everything I am... just to escape?"

The mark on her arm flared, and Sarah screamed as she was searing pain, shot through her body. She collapsed to the ground, her limbs trembling as the rift's pull grew stronger. She could feel herself being drawn closer, her body losing substance as the edges of her form began to blur.

"No," she gasped, her nails digging into the ground as she fought against the pull. "I won't let you take me."

The rift's voices turned mocking; their whispers laced with dark amusement. "You can't hold on forever. The gateway's pull is inevitable."

Sarah gritted her teeth, her determination flaring even as her strength waned. "I'm stronger than you think," she spat, her voice shaking but fierce.

The ground beneath her rippled violently, and the light from the rift grew blinding. She closed her eyes, clinging to the memories that anchored her—Liam's laugh, the warmth of the sun on her face, the feeling of paint beneath her fingers. They were hers, and she wouldn't let this place take them.

When she opened her eyes, she was still on the ground, the rift looming before her. The mark on her arm pulsed faintly, its light dimmer now, as though the dimension had momentarily relented. Sarah took a shaky breath, her body trembling with exhaustion.

The rift's whispers quieted, but its presence remained oppressive, a constant reminder of the choice she would eventually have to make.

"This isn't over," she said, her voice barely more than a whisper.

She forced herself to her feet, swaying unsteadily as she faced the rift. "You're not going to win."

The dimension seemed to pulse in response, the air around her thick with anticipation. Sarah took a step back, her resolve unshaken even as the weight of the alien world pressed down on her.

The fight wasn't over. Not yet.

CHAPTER 19: THE RIFT'S HUNGER

The alien dimension bore down on Sarah like a tidal wave, relentless and overwhelming. Every inch of her body ached as she staggered forward, the ground beneath her feet rippling with each step. The storm of swirling colors raged closer, flashes of light illuminating the grotesque beauty of the rift ahead. The mark on her arm burned brighter than ever, its veins of light now spreading across her shoulder and chest, a glowing map of the alien world's influence.

"It's pulling me apart," she whispered, her voice hoarse. She clutched her arm, feeling the heat radiating from the mark. "If I don't stop it soon, there won't be anything left of me to save."

But the rift's pull was unyielding. It wasn't just her body that it tugged at—it was her mind, her memories, her very sense of self. Each step closer felt like peeling away another layer of who she was, leaving her exposed and vulnerable.

The voices returned, rising from the rift like a chorus of whispers. They layered over each other, some soft and coaxing, others sharp and demanding.

"You carry so much weight," they said. "We can take it away. All of it. Step through and be free."

Sarah clenched her teeth, forcing herself to keep walking even as the voices grew louder, more insistent. "Freedom?" she spat, her voice trembling. "You mean becoming… one of those things?"

Her eyes darted to the shapes within the rift. Some were serene, their forms glowing softly as they drifted in the swirling light. Others were monstrous, their bodies twisted and grotesque, a horrifying blend of human and alien features. Faces flickered in and out of the chaos, mouths moving soundlessly, their eyes wide with something between ecstasy and despair.

A flash of light erupted from the rift, and Sarah's vision shifted. She found herself standing on the edge of eternity, gazing into a boundless expanse of shifting colors and infinite possibilities. It was beautiful, terrifying, and utterly incomprehensible. The dimension stretched on forever, its vastness pressing down on her like a physical weight.

"This is what awaits," the voices whispered. "A higher existence. A release from all that binds you. You can be so much more."

The vision twisted, and Sarah saw herself among the beings within the rift. Her body shimmered and dissolved; her features unrecognizable as she became part of the alien realm. There was no pain, no fear, no grief—only an overwhelming sense of peace.

But there was also nothing left of her. No laughter, no memories of Liam, no dreams of the life she'd fought so hard to hold onto. She was a fragment, a flicker of light in an endless sea of others.

"Is this what you want?" the voices asked. "To transcend? To let go of everything that hurts?"

"No," Sarah whispered, tears streaming down her face. "No, I won't give you that."

The mark on her arm flared, and a wave of searing pain shot through her body. She collapsed to her knees, her nails digging into the rippling ground as she fought to stay grounded. The rift's pull grew stronger, and she could feel herself being drawn closer, her body losing substance as the edges of her form began to blur.

"You're slipping," the voices said, their tone mocking now. "You can't resist forever."

"I won't let you take me," Sarah growled, her voice trembling but fierce. She gripped the ground beneath her, the cool, rippling surface anchoring her in place. Memories flashed through her mind—Liam's laugh, the smell of fresh paint in her studio, the feeling of sunlight on her skin. They were hers, and she wouldn't let this place take them away.

The rift's light grew blinding, the swirling shapes within moving faster, more chaotically. The voices rose to a crescendo, their overlapping whispers turning into a deafening roar. Sarah screamed; the sound swallowed by the cacophony around her. Her body trembled, every muscle straining as she fought against the rift's pull.

But then, the voices shifted. For a moment, they sounded almost... pleading.

"Let go," they said, softer now. "Let us take the pain. You don't have to fight anymore."

Sarah's resolve wavered, the temptation to give in tugging at her heart. The thought of release, of freedom from the weight she carried, was almost too much to resist. But she closed her eyes, clinging to the one truth that anchored her.

"I am Sarah," she whispered. "I am human. I am me."

The ground beneath her steadied, the light from the rift dimming slightly. Sarah opened her eyes, her breaths coming in ragged gasps. She was still on the edge, the rift looming before her like a living thing. The mark on her arm pulsed faintly, its light no longer spreading but still glowing with an unsettling warmth.

The rift's whispers quieted, their tone shifting from mocking to something almost... curious.

"You are strong," they said, their words carrying a hint of respect.

"But strength will only take you so far."

Sarah forced herself to her feet, her legs trembling beneath her. She faced the rift, her resolve unshaken despite the exhaustion that weighed her down.

"You're not going to win," she said, her voice steady. "Not today. Not ever."

The rift pulsed once, the shapes within it slowing their chaotic dance. The dimension seemed to hold its breath, the air around her thick with anticipation. Sarah took a step back, her eyes never leaving the rift as she prepared for whatever came next.

The fight wasn't over. Not yet.

CHAPTER 20: THE KEEPER RETURNS

The air thickened with tension as Sarah forced herself away from the rift's edge, her breaths shallow and labored. Each step felt like wading through quicksand, the dimension pressing down on her as though it knew she had defied its pull. The mark on her arm pulsed faintly, its glow no longer spreading but still ominously alive. The rift loomed behind her, silent for the first time since she had arrived, its quiet hum filled with anticipation.

And then, the Keeper returned.

Its form materialized from the swirling storm; more alien than before. Its body shifted constantly, a fluid amalgamation of shadow and light, impossible to pin down. Tendrils of energy snaked out from its core, reaching and retreating in an unsettling rhythm. It stood taller now, its presence overwhelming, filling the space with a gravity that made Sarah's knees tremble.

"You've resisted longer than most," the Keeper said, its voice a symphony of overlapping tones. "That's admirable. But it's time to decide."

Sarah steadied herself, her fists clenching at her sides. "I already made my decision," she said, her voice sharp despite the weariness in her bones. "I'm not stepping through."

The Keeper tilted its head, the motion both curious and predatory. "You misunderstand," it said. "Resisting is not the same as choosing. And this place... it requires a choice."

The Keeper extended a hand, its fingers stretching unnaturally as they reached toward her. Sarah stepped back, her breath hitching as the mark on her arm flared in response.

"What do you want from me?" she demanded, her voice trembling.

The Keeper's form flickered, its tendrils twisting in agitation. "What we always want: to guide. To transform. The cottage exists not to punish, but to save. It finds those who carry the weight of their world and offers them release. Freedom."

Sarah's chest tightened as the words sank in. "Freedom?" she echoed, her voice laced with disbelief. "By turning them into... whatever those things are in the rift?"

The Keeper's form shifted closer, the light from its core casting eerie shadows across Sarah's face. "Those who step through transcend," it said. "They shed their fear, their pain, their regrets. They become part of something greater."

"They lose themselves," Sarah countered, her voice rising. "Their memories, their identities—gone. That's not freedom. That's annihilation."

The Keeper's tendrils coiled inward, its form flickering as though the dimension itself bristled at her words. "The cottage does not take," it said. "It offers. Only those who resist too long are absorbed... their essence feeding the gateway's power."

Sarah's stomach churned. "You mean if I keep fighting, I'll end up part of this place anyway?"

"Yes," the Keeper said, its voice devoid of malice, almost pitying. "But not as you fear. To resist is to delay the inevitable. The longer you fight, the more you weaken, until there is nothing left to preserve. The choice is simple: step through willingly and find peace, or struggle and be consumed."

"There has to be another way," Sarah said, her voice desperate. "I can't just give up who I am."

The Keeper's form stilled, its shifting edges momentarily stabilizing. "You carry so much pain," it said softly. "The guilt of your brother's death. The ache of your own failures. The weight of it crushes you, yet you cling to it as if it defines you. Why?"

Sarah's breath caught, the words striking a nerve. "Because it does define me," she said, her voice breaking. "Every mistake, every loss, every scar—they're part of who I am. If I let them go, what's left?"

The Keeper tilted its head again, its tendrils unfurling. "You fear emptiness," it said. "But emptiness can be filled. The rift offers more than escape. It offers transformation. Creation. Eternity."

The Keeper extended its hand again, its tendrils glowing faintly as they reached for her. "Step through," it urged. "Embrace what lies beyond. Or continue to fight, and let the rift decide your fate."

Sarah stared at the outstretched hand, her pulse roaring in her ears. The mark on her arm burned, the veins of light pulsing in time with the rift's rhythm. Every instinct screamed at her to run, but there was nowhere to go. The dimension surrounded her, its oppressive presence pressing closer with every passing second.

"I need more time," she said finally, her voice barely more than a whisper.

The Keeper's tendrils paused, its form flickering as though considering her words. "Time is a luxury the rift does not grant freely," it said. "But you have earned this moment. Use it wisely."

With that, the Keeper dissolved into the air, its form unraveling into threads of light and shadow. The dimension fell silent, the storm of colors dimming slightly as the rift's hum grew softer. Sarah stood alone, her chest heaving as she tried to steady her thoughts.

The choice loomed before her, heavy and inescapable. But for now,

DINESH DECKKER

the fight isn't over.
Not yet.

CHAPTER 21: CONFRONTING THE RIFT

The silence after the Keeper's departure was almost worse than its presence. The rift loomed ahead, its glow pulsating in slow, deliberate rhythms. The storm of swirling colors around Sarah had stilled, as though the dimension itself waited, watching. She took a shaky breath, her hands trembling as she stared at the mark on her arm. The glow had dimmed slightly, but it remained alive, a tether she couldn't break.

"It's not over," she whispered to herself, her voice barely audible in the oppressive quiet. "Not yet."

But even as she said the words, the rift responded. The hum grew louder, a low, resonant tone that reverberated through her chest. The air thickened, and the edges of her vision blurred. Before she could take another step, the world shifted.

She was back in her childhood home.

The sudden familiarity made her stomach lurch. The living room was exactly as she remembered: the faded floral couch, the coffee table littered with Liam's comic books, the faint smell of lavender air freshener. For a moment, she let herself believe it was real.

Then she heard the voice.

"Sarah."

She turned slowly, her breath catching in her throat. Liam stood in the doorway, his hands in his pockets, his face shadowed but unmistakable. He looked just as he had the last time, she'd seen him alive—young, hopeful, and full of life. But there was something in his eyes, a flicker of accusation that sent a chill down her spine.

"Liam?" she whispered, her voice trembling. "Is it really you?"

He stepped closer, his movements slow and deliberate. "You had the power to save me," he said, his voice low and heavy. "But you chose not to. Why, Sarah? Why did you leave me?"

Her chest tightened, tears welling up in her eyes. "No," she said, shaking her head. "That's not true. I didn't leave you. I tried... I tried to save you."

Liam's expression darkened, his features twisting with anger. "You knew how much I needed you," he said, his voice rising. "But you weren't there. You let me die, Sarah. You let me down."

The room began to warp, the walls bending inward as shadows crept across the floor. Liam's form flickered, his face shifting between anger and despair. "You carry it every day," he said, his voice overlapping with itself. "The guilt. Regret. You know I'm right."

Sarah stumbled back, her hands clutching at her head. The shadows clawed at her mind, pulling at the memories she had tried so hard to suppress. She saw the day of Liam's death, the moments leading up to it, the crushing weight of her failure.

"Stop it," she said, her voice breaking. "You're not him. You're just another trick."

"A trick?" Liam's voice softened, his form stabilizing as he stepped closer. "No, Sarah. I'm the truth you've been running from. The truth you're too afraid to face."

Her knees buckled, and she fell to the floor, tears streaming down her face. The shadows pressed closer, suffocating her. But beneath the fear, a spark of defiance burned.

"You're not taking this from me," she whispered, her voice trembling but growing stronger. She looked up, meeting the illusion's gaze. "I loved you, Liam. I still do. But I can't live in the past anymore."

The shadows faltered, the room shuddering as cracks appeared in the walls. Liam's form flickered, his expression shifting to one of sorrow.

"You don't have to," he said softly, his voice almost human again. "Just let go."

"No," Sarah said firmly, pushing herself to her feet. "I'll carry it. I'll carry all of it, because it's mine. It's what makes me who I am."

The illusion shattered; the pieces dissolved into the air. Sarah stood alone in silence, her chest heaving as she wiped her tears away. The mark on her arm pulsed faintly, its glow dimmer now, as though weakened by her defiance.

For the first time, she felt a sense of control. The rift's pull lessened, and the oppressive weight of the dimension lifted slightly. She took a deep breath, her mind clearer than it had been in days.

But the reprieve was short-lived. The rift's hum grew louder, its light darkening as though responding to her defiance. The ground beneath her feet trembled, and the air grew colder, sharper.

Sarah clenched her fists, her resolve hardening. "If you think I'm giving up now," she said, her voice steady, "you're wrong."

CHAPTER 22: THE RIFT'S FURY

The air in the dimension seemed to split open with a deafening groan as the rift responded to Sarah's defiance. The ground beneath her rippled violently, its surface cracking and splintering like glass. The once-still storm erupted, colors flashing erratically as the space around her twisted and convulsed. She stumbled, barely keeping her balance as the cottage itself began to contort.

The walls of the cottage—those familiar, warped barriers that had once felt like a trap—buckled inward toward the rift. Their groans echoed like the last breaths of a dying beast, and the ceiling bowed as if trying to escape the pull. Pieces of plaster and wood rained down, vanishing into the swirling light before they hit the ground. The cottage was being consumed.

Sarah's pulse pounded in her ears as she fought to keep her footing. She turned, her eyes scanning the room as alien shapes began to emerge from the rift's glow. Tall, gaunt figures stepped forward, their forms shifting and flickering like shadows caught in a strobe light. They moved with unnatural grace, their hollow eyes fixed on her. Watching. Waiting.

"The cottage…" she muttered, her voice trembling. "It's falling apart."

"No," a voice corrected, low and resonant. "It is returning."

The Keeper emerged from the storm; its form more defined but infinitely more alien. Tendrils of light and shadow swirled around it, coiling like serpents. Its face was a shifting void, impossible to focus on. The gravity of its presence pressed down on Sarah, making her knees tremble.

"Resisting won't save you," the Keeper said, its voice layered with calm and menace. "It will only destroy you."

Sarah forced herself to stand tall, clenching her fists as she faced the Keeper. "Then I'll take it all down with me," she said, her voice steady despite the storm raging around her.

The Keeper tilted its head, a faint glimmer of amusement rippling through its form. "Bold words from a fading light," it said. "But words alone cannot undo what has already begun."

The ground beneath her shifted again, throwing her off balance. She hit the floor hard, the breath knocked from her lungs. Around her, the alien figures moved closer, their silent stares unyielding. The rift's pull intensified, and she felt it deep in her core—a force tugging at her very essence, trying to unmake her.

Sarah's hand brushed against the glowing mark on her arm, and a spark of pain shot through her. She winced but froze as her fingers traced the intricate lines. There was a pattern there, one she hadn't noticed before. The lines weren't random; they formed symbols, shapes she had seen carved into the walls of the cottage and in the notebook left behind by the previous visitor.

"The mark," she whispered, her eyes widening. "It's connected."

The Keeper watched her, its tendrils coiling tighter. "The mark binds you," it said. "It is the bridge between you and the gateway. You cannot sever it. It is part of you now."

But Sarah's mind raced, piecing together fragments of memory and instinct. She recalled the journal's frantic scribbles, the warnings and symbols etched into the walls. The mark wasn't just a tether—it was a key.

The cottage groaned again, its walls buckled further as pieces of it vanished into the rift. The alien figures stepped closer; their hollow gazes unrelenting. Sarah scrambled to her feet, her heart pounding as she clutched her arm. The symbols burned brighter, their glow pulsating in time with the rift's rhythm.

"I'll find a way," she said, her voice fierce. "I'll stop this."

The Keeper's form rippled; its tone laced with pity. "You cannot stop what is eternal," it said. "The gateway does not close. It does not yield. It consumes."

Sarah ignored the Keeper, her focus sharpening as she studied the mark. The lines intersected in precise patterns, forming a network of energy that seemed to resonate with the rift. Her fingers traced the edges, and she felt a faint vibration beneath her skin.

"This is it," she muttered. "This is how I fight back."

The ground trembled violently, and a deafening roar erupted from the rift. The alien figures froze, their heads tilting in unison as if sensing her intent. The Keeper's form shifted, its tendrils writhing in agitation.

"What are you doing?" it demanded, its voice sharp for the first time.

Sarah didn't answer. Her fingers pressed harder against the mark, her mind racing as she tried to decipher the patterns. The lines glowed brighter, the pain in her arm intensifying, but she refused to stop.

The rift's light darkened, its pull growing stronger as the dimension itself seemed to resist her efforts. The storm of colors swirled faster, and the air crackled with energy. But Sarah's resolve hardened.

"If you think I'm giving up," she said through gritted teeth, "you don't know me at all."

The Keeper's form flickered, its tendrils stretching toward her as the storm reached a fever pitch. Sarah's vision blurred, but she kept her focus on the mark, her determination blazing against the chaos.

The rift roared, and the dimension trembled, teetering on the edge of collapse.

CHAPTER 23: THE FINAL BATTLE

The air crackled with energy as Sarah gritted her teeth, her fingers trembling as they pressed against the glowing mark on her arm. The rift roared behind her, its pull intensifying as the dimension fought to maintain its grip. Around her, the cottage's walls groaned and splintered, shards of wood and plaster dissolving into the swirling void. The alien figures encircled her, their hollow eyes unblinking as they watched.

This is it, she thought, her heart pounding. *It's all or nothing now.*

The mark burned like fire under her touch, but Sarah didn't stop. She traced the intricate patterns, her mind racing to piece together the symbols and their meaning. The lines intersected in ways that mirrored the carvings she'd seen in the cottage walls, each one resonating with a faint hum that matched the rhythm of the rift. It wasn't just a connection—it was a conduit.

"You won't take me," she muttered through gritted teeth. "Not without a fight."

The rift's pull grew stronger, and Sarah felt her body lurch toward it. She planted her feet firmly, her boots digging into the rippling ground as she fought against the force. The alien figures moved closer, their forms flickering like mirages, their presence suffocating.

"Sarah."

The Keeper's voice sliced through the chaos, calm and unyielding. It stood at the edge of the rift, its form shimmering with tendrils of light and shadow. "You could have been more," it said, its tone tinged with something almost like regret. "Why do you choose to remain tethered to pain?"

Sarah looked up, her eyes blazing with defiance. "Because pain is part of being human," she said, her voice steady despite the storm raging around her. "It's messy and hard, but it's real. And I'd rather feel all of it than lose myself to you."

The Keeper's tendrils coiled tighter, its form flickering as the rift roared behind it. "Your resolve is admirable," it said, "but futile. The gateway cannot be closed. It is eternal, as am I."

Sarah's grip on the mark tightened, her fingers digging into her skin as she focused all her energy on the symbols. She could feel the vibration beneath her fingertips intensify, the hum growing louder. The lines glowed brighter, pulsating in rhythm with her heartbeat.

"We'll see about that," she said.

The cottage's collapse accelerated. Walls folded inward, revealing endless voids of light and shadow. The air buzzed with energy, a deafening roar filling the space as the rift began to consume everything around it. The alien figures stepped back; their hollow eyes fixed on Sarah as if awaiting her next move.

Sarah's breaths came in ragged gasps, her body trembling from the effort. The mark burned brighter, the pain spreading through her arm like wildfire. But she refused to stop. She closed her eyes, focusing on the memories that anchored her: Liam's laugh, the feeling of paint under her fingers, the sunlight warming her face. They were hers, and she wouldn't let the rift take them.

"I am Sarah," she whispered. "I am human. And I'm enough."

The mark flared, and a surge of energy shot through her body. The symbols glowed with a blinding light, their intricate patterns shifting as they resonated with the rift. The alien figures recoiled, their forms dissolving into the storm as the ground beneath them cracked and splintered.

The Keeper's tendrils lashed out, stretching toward her in a final attempt to stop her. "You cannot defy eternity," it said, its voice a low growl. "You will only destroy yourself."

Sarah opened her eyes, her gaze locked on the Keeper. "Better me than you," she said.

With a final burst of strength, she pressed her hand against the mark, channeling all her energy into it. The light intensified, the symbols shifting and breaking apart as the rift's pulling began to falter. The storm around her grew wild, the colors swirling faster as the dimension trembled.

The rift let out a deafening roar, its edges collapsing inward as the light dimmed. The alien figures vanished, their forms dissolved into the void. The Keeper's tendrils recoiled, its form flickering violently as it staggered back toward the rift.

"This is not the end," it said, its voice echoing as it was pulled into the collapsing gateway. "The gateway cannot be destroyed. It will return."

Sarah watched as the Keeper disappeared, its final words swallowed by the storm. The rift collapsed inward, its light fading until only darkness remained. The dimension around her began to dissolve, the ground beneath her feet crumbling into nothingness.

She fell to her knees, her body trembling with exhaustion. The mark on her arm flickered, its glow fading until it was nothing more than a faint scar. The air grew still, the oppressive weight of the dimension lifting as silence settled over space.

Sarah closed her eyes, her breaths shallow as she let herself collapse onto the ground. The fight was over, but the cost of her victory lingered in the emptiness around her. She didn't know what would come next, but for the first time, she felt a fragile sense of peace.

And then, everything dissolved into light.

CHAPTER 24: THE AFTERMATH

The first thing Sarah noticed was the quiet. It was an unnatural silence, heavy and absolute, as though the world itself had stopped holding its breath. She opened her eyes slowly, her body aching with deep, bone-deep exhaustion. The ground beneath her was damp and soft earth, not the shimmering, rippling surface of the alien dimension. Above her, the sky was a pale, muted gray, the tops of the trees swaying gently in a breeze she couldn't feel.

She was back.

For a moment, Sarah lay there, her chest rising and falling in shallow, uneven breaths. The memories of the rift and the Keeper lingered at the edges of her mind, vivid and surreal. She closed her eyes, half-expecting to wake back in the shifting chaos of the dimension, but when she opened them again, the forest remained.

The cottage was gone.

She sat up slowly, every muscle protesting the movement. The forest stretched around her, eerily still. The underbrush was undisturbed, the trees tall and ancient, their branches weaving a canopy that muted the light. It was as if nothing had ever happened.

"It's over," she whispered, her voice rasping against the silence. "It has to be over."

But even as she said the words, a knot of unease twisted in her stomach. Her hand drifted to her arm, her fingers brushing the faint scar where the mark had been. The skin was smooth and unbroken, but she could still feel it—an echo of the burning light, the connection that had tethered her to the rift. It was gone, but it wasn't. Not entirely.

The walk out of the forest felt longer than it should have. Each step was weighed down by the heaviness in her chest, her mind replaying fragments of what she had seen and felt. The faces in the rift, the Keeper's final words, the moment the dimension had collapsed around her. She pushed the memories aside, focusing instead on the crunch of leaves underfoot, the steady rhythm of her breathing.

When she reached the edge of the forest, the world opened up before her. The small dirt road she'd driven down felt foreign, its familiarity tinged with a sense of displacement. Her car sat where she'd left it, dusted with leaves and dirt as though no time had passed at all.

She hesitated, her fingers brushing the car door handle. The air around her felt lighter here, but it carried a faint hum, almost imperceptible, like the lingering echo of a storm long gone.

Back home, silence followed her. The apartment was exactly as she'd left it: the cluttered table by the window, the half-finished painting on the easel, the stack of unopened letters on the counter. Yet it all felt wrong, as though the life she'd stepped back into belonged to someone else.

She spent hours sitting on the couch, her knees pulled to her chest, staring at the blank wall. The events in the cottage and the dimension played in her mind like a broken record. She remembered the Keeper's voice, the pull of the rift, the way the mark on her arm had burned like it was alive. She could still feel it sometimes, a phantom heat that made her skin crawl.

"It's gone," she whispered to herself. "But why doesn't it feel over?"

Days turned into weeks, and Sarah tried to return to her routine. She painted, she went for walks, she answered the occasional phone call. But the unease never left her. Small, subtle things began to unsettle her: the way the shadows in her apartment seemed to stretch just a little too long at dusk, the faint whispers she sometimes thought she heard in the wind, the way her reflection in the mirror felt… off.

One night, she stood in front of the mirror, studying her face. Dark circles hung under her eyes, her skin pale and drawn. She reached up, brushing her hair away from her forehead, and froze. For a split second, she thought she saw something move in her reflection—a flicker of light, a shimmer that reminded her too much of the alien dimension.

Her heart raced as she stepped back, her hand clenching the edge of the sink. The scar on her arm prickled faintly, a phantom sensation that sent chills down her spine. She turned away, her breathing shallow, but the image lingered in her mind.

She couldn't shake the feeling that the cottage's influence hadn't truly left her. It was subtle, like a shadow lurking at the edges of her vision, always just out of reach. She began to notice patterns she hadn't before: symbols etched faintly into the bark of trees on her walks, the way streetlights flickered when she passed beneath them, the faint hum in her ears when she lay in bed at night.

One evening, as she stood by her window, staring out at the city below, she felt the scar on her arm burn faintly. She looked down, expecting to see smooth skin, but the faint outline of the mark glowed softly, pulsing in rhythm with her heartbeat.

The wind outside whispered through the cracked window, carrying a sound that made her blood run cold. It was faint, almost imperceptible, but unmistakable.

A whisper.

Her name.

Sarah turned away from the window, her chest tight as she sank to the floor. She pressed her hands against her ears, willing the sound to stop, but it lingered, a haunting reminder of what she'd left behind—or what had followed her home.

In the weeks that followed, she tried to find meaning in what had happened, to piece together the fragments of her experience into something she could understand. But the memories were fractured, slipping through her fingers like water. She began to wonder if she would ever be free of the rift, or if it had taken more from her than she realized.

One morning, as she stood in front of her mirror, she stared into her own eyes, searching for something—anything—familiar. For a moment, her reflection stared back, perfectly ordinary.

And then it changed.

The shimmer returned, faint and fleeting, but enough to send a shiver down her spine. Her reflection's eyes glowed faintly, the same eerie light she'd seen in the dimension. It was gone in an instant, but the mark on her arm burned in response, its glow brighter than before.

Sarah stepped back, her heart pounding. She pressed her hand against the scar, her fingers trembling. The air around her seemed to hum, a low, steady vibration that felt like a heartbeat.

She closed her eyes, drawing a deep, shaky breath. When she opened them again, her reflection was normal. But the lingering unease remained.

The cottage was gone. The rift was closed. But its shadow still clung to her, a reminder that some doors, once opened, are never truly shut.

CHAPTER 25: THE LEGACY OF THE RIFT

The rain fell in a steady rhythm, a soft patter against the canopy of trees that loomed over the narrow dirt path. Somewhere deep in the forest, a figure moved with deliberate care, their flashlight beam slicing through the darkness. The light caught on something—a small, weathered leather journal lying in the underbrush, its edges damp and curling.

The figure knelt, their gloved hand brushing the cover. The journal felt unnaturally warm despite the chill in the air. They hesitated before opening it, flipping to the first page. The handwriting was shaky, the words scrawled in haste:

It's alive. And it's waiting.

A shiver ran down their spine. They glanced around the forest, as though expecting something to leap from the shadows. The air felt heavier now, the silence almost oppressive. Flipping further into the journal, they found crude sketches of a cottage, symbols etched into the walls, and fragments of text that made little sense.

The cottage chooses.

It sees your pain.

Beware the rift.

The figure closed the journal abruptly, their breath hitching. They tucked it into their bag and rose to their feet, casting one last look at the shadows that seemed to stretch unnaturally long.

Across town, Sarah sat on the floor of her apartment, the room dimly lit by a single lamp. In front of her lay her own journal, its pages spread open to the chaotic notes she'd scribbled after escaping the rift. The ink had smudged in places where her tears had fallen, but the words were still legible. The memories were raw and unyielding, etched into her mind as deeply as the faint scar on her arm.

She picked up the journal, her fingers tracing the edges of the pages. The thought of destroying it had crossed her mind countless times. It would be so easy—a match, a flicker of flame, and it would all be gone. But every time she'd tried, something held her back. The weight of the experience, the lingering connection to the cottage, wouldn't let her let go.

"Would they even believe me?" she muttered to herself, her voice hollow. "Would I... want them to?"

Her eyes drifted to the faint glow of the scar on her arm. It was barely noticeable now, but in the dim light, it pulsed faintly, a reminder that the rift's shadow hadn't entirely left her. She closed the journal and set it on the floor, staring at it for a long moment.

The rain outside intensified, drumming against the windows. Sarah rose to her feet, walking to the window to watch the water streak down the glass. The city below was a blur of lights and movement, but it all felt distant, like watching a world she no longer belonged to.

A whisper cut through the noise of the rain. It was faint, almost imperceptible, but it sent a chill down her spine. She turned sharply, her eyes scanning the apartment, but nothing was there. The whisper came again, clearer this time.

"Come back."

Her chest tightened as the voice echoed in her mind, unmistakable in its familiarity. It was the same voice she'd heard in the dimension, the same one that had lured her toward the rift. She backed away from the window, her hands trembling.

"No," she whispered, her voice cracking. "You're gone. I closed it. You're gone."

But the whisper didn't stop. It wrapped around her, weaving through her thoughts like a thread she couldn't unravel. The scar on her arm burned faintly, and she clutched it, willing the sensation to fade.

In the forest, the figure who had found the journal paused, their flashlight flickering. They glanced down at the bag slung over their shoulder, the weight of the journal feeling heavier than it should. The air around them seemed to hum, a faint vibration that resonated deep in their chest.

They turned, their eyes catching a glimpse of something in the distance. It was faint, but unmistakable: the silhouette of a cottage, its windows glowing softly in the rain. For a moment, they stood frozen, torn between curiosity and an overwhelming urge to run.

The hum grew louder, and the figure took a hesitant step forward.

Back in her apartment, Sarah stared at the journal on the floor, her mind racing. She wanted to leave it behind, to walk away and never think about the cottage or the rift again. But something in her refused to let go. She reached down, her fingers brushing the cover, and felt a jolt of warmth—the same unnatural heat she'd felt in the forest.

She stood abruptly, crossing the room and shoving the journal into a drawer. Slamming it shut, she leaned against the wall, her breaths shallow. The whisper had stopped, but the unease lingered, coiling around her like a shadow she couldn't shake.

Outside, the rain slowed, the city falling into a quiet lull. Sarah glanced at the drawer one last time before turning away, grabbing her coat and stepping out into the night. The air was crisp and cool, the kind of air that felt like it could cleanse something from your soul.

She walked aimlessly, her thoughts heavy but her steps purposeful. She didn't know where she was going, but she needed to move, to escape the weight pressing down on her.

As she reached the edge of the park, she paused, looking out over the darkened trees. The shadows stretched long and deep, and for a moment, she thought she saw something flicker at the edge of her vision. A light. A shimmer.

She shook her head, tearing her gaze away. "It's over," she said to herself. "It has to be."

Far away, in the depths of the forest, the cottage stood waiting. Its walls glowed faintly in the darkness, its windows reflecting a light that didn't come from this world. Inside, the air was still, the silence unbroken. But on the table by the fireplace, a new journal lay open, its pages blank and waiting.

And outside, the figure approached, their steps slow but deliberate. The cottage's light pulsed once, welcoming them home.

AFTERWORD

Writing *The Cottage Within* has been a journey into the unknown—both for the characters and for me as its author. This story began as a spark of curiosity about the boundaries between reality and illusion, between what we fear and what we long for. Along the way, it became an exploration of grief, resilience, and the choices that define us.

Sarah's journey through the rift is, at its heart, a reflection of the human experience: grappling with the weight of our past while daring to imagine what lies beyond. Her strength, her flaws, and her determination to face the shadows that threaten to consume her are what make her story not just one of survival, but of transformation.

To my wife, Subhashini, and my daughter, Sasha—thank you for being my anchor in this vast, creative expanse. Your love and support are the foundation on which all my stories are built.

To you, the reader: thank you for stepping into the cottage and walking alongside Sarah. The shadows within us are daunting, but they are also where we discover the light. If this story has resonated with you, if it has sparked even a small moment of reflection, then it has served its purpose.

Some doors remain open, lingering in the corners of our minds. But perhaps that is where the greatest stories are born.

With gratitude,

D. Deckker

ACKNOWLEDGEMENT

Writing *The Cottage Within* has been an incredible journey, and I am deeply grateful to the people who supported me along the way.

To my wife, Subhashini, and my daughter, Sasha—your love and encouragement have been my guiding light. Thank you for believing in me, even when the shadows seemed too daunting.

To my editor, whose sharp insights and dedication helped refine this story into what it is today—thank you for pushing me to go deeper and trust the process.

To my close friends and early readers, thank you for your honest feedback and unwavering support. Your enthusiasm and thoughtful critiques gave me the confidence to continue.

To every teacher, writer, and storyteller who has ever inspired me, and to the readers who step into this story—this book exists because of you. Thank you for sharing in this journey.

Finally, to the unknown—the mysteries that lie within and beyond—thank you for sparking the imagination that led to this story. May we always have the courage to open new doors.

With gratitude,
D. Deckker

ABOUT THE AUTHOR

D. Deckker

Dinesh Deckker is a multifaceted author and educator with a rich academic background and extensive experience in creative writing and education. Holding a BSc Hons in Computer Science, a BA (Hons), and an MBA from prestigious institutions in the UK and Cuurrently reading for PhD. Dinesh has dedicated his career to blending technology, education, and literature.

He has further honed his writing skills through a variety of specialized courses. His qualifications include:

Children Acquiring Literacy Naturally from UC Santa Cruz, USA
Creative Writing Specialization from Wesleyan University, USA
Writing for Young Readers Commonwealth Education Trust
Introduction to Early Childhood from The State University of New York
Introduction to Psychology from Yale University
Academic English: Writing Specialization University of California, Irvine,
Writing and Editing Specialization from University of Michigan
Writing and Editing: Word Choice University of Michigan
Sharpened Visions: A Poetry Workshop from CalArts, USA
Grammar and Punctuation from University of California, Irvine,

USA
Teaching Writing Specialization from Johns Hopkins University
Advanced Writing from University of California, Irvine, USA
English for Journalism from University of Pennsylvania, USA
Creative Writing: The Craft of Character from Wesleyan University, USA
Creative Writing: The Craft of Setting from Wesleyan University
Creative Writing: The Craft of Plot from Wesleyan University, USA
Creative Writing: The Craft of Style from Wesleyan University, USA

Dinesh's diverse educational background and commitment to lifelong learning have equipped him with a deep understanding of various writing styles and educational techniques. His works often reflect his passion for storytelling, education, and technology, making him a versatile and engaging author.

BOOKS BY THIS AUTHOR

Red Suit Killer: Christmas Serial Killer Story

The 'Red Suit Killer' has turned Christmas into a nightmare, targeting men dressed as Santa Claus and leaving behind grotesque scenes that transform beloved holiday symbols into messages of vengeance. With the clock ticking toward Christmas Eve, Detective Sarah Vale must unravel cryptic clues and confront her own haunted past to stop a killer who knows the season's darkest truths.

The Titan Expedition: A Sci-Fi Adventure Beyond Saturn

In the year 2078, humanity intercepts an enigmatic signal emanating from Titan, Saturn's largest moon. Persistent, intricate, and intelligent, the signal sparks a high-stakes mission to uncover its origin—a journey that could change the course of human history forever.

Led by the determined Captain Elena Vega, the crew of the spacecraft Odyssey embarks on a perilous expedition to Titan. Each member of the team—brilliant scientists, seasoned explorers, and a corporate insider with hidden motives—must confront their own fears, secrets, and ambitions as they venture into the alien depths of space.

The Yule Fiend: Christmas Tale Of Fear, Folklore,

And Redemption

When Ingrid returns to the remote Nordic village of Frostmark for the holidays, she expects little more than awkward family reunions and icy nights. Instead, she finds herself drawn into a chilling legend whispered through generations: the Yule Fiend, a monstrous creature haunting the forests, demanding ritualistic offerings to keep its wrath at bay.

But this year, the Fiend grows restless. A friend's sudden disappearance sets Ingrid on a dangerous path to uncover the truth behind the creature's curse and the village's deeply rooted traditions. With ancient hymns, forgotten lore, and her own courage as her only weapons, Ingrid must confront not only the Fiend but also the shadows of her own past.

Santa's Naughty List: A Twisted Christmas Horror Story

North Pole Wonderland was once a place of joy and cheer—a magical amusement park that celebrated everything about Christmas. Now, it's abandoned, haunted by shadows of a dark history no one dares to remember. When Eve and her friends break into the park on a dare, they awaken something far more sinister than they ever imagined—a monstrous version of Santa Claus who insists they are all on his "naughty list."

Made in the USA
Columbia, SC
22 January 2025